THE MOST DANGEROUS SCORE

Michael Hardcastle was born in Huddersfield in Yorkshire. After leaving school he served in the Royal Army Educational Corps before embarking on a career in journalism, working in a number of roles for provincial daily newspapers from reporter to chief feature writer.

He has written more than one hundred and forty children's books since his first was published in 1966, but still finds time to visit schools and colleges all over Britain to talk about books and writing. In 1988 he was awarded an MBE in recognition of his services to children's books. He is married and lives in Beverley, Yorkshire.

by the same author

The Fastest Bowler in the World

One Kick

Own Goal

Quake

Second Chance

Please Come Home

in the Goal Kings series

The Most Dangerous Score

Michael Hardcastle

Goal Kings
BOOK SIX

ff

faber and faber

First published in 2001
by Faber and Faber Limited
3 Queen Square London WC1N 3AU

Typeset by Avon Dataset, Bidford-on-Avon, Warwickshire
Printed and bound in England by Mackays of Chatham PLC,
Chatham, Kent

© Michael Hardcastle, 2001

A CIP record for this book
is available from the British Library

ISBN 0-571-20559-3

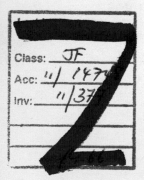

2 4 6 8 10 9 7 5 3 1

Contents

1 Love Letters

Kieren glanced round, trying to make sure that no one who knew him would see what he was doing. But the rush of pupils leaving Rodale High School at the end of the day was such that hardly anyone was in an inquisitive mood. So no one really noticed Kieren turn off the long corridor and slip into one of the language laboratories. Even as he pushed the door to behind him with his foot he was tearing open the envelope his girlfriend Andrea had passed to him fifty-five minutes earlier.

The interval before he could open it in private had seemed like a lifetime. Even though they saw each other every day, and sometimes even had hours together on their own, the recent development of writing love letters to each other in school was yet another exciting phase of their friendship. What would she be telling him this time?

He had read only a couple of lines when someone pushed the door open and announced: 'Hey, thought it was you sneaking in here! What're you up to? Not learning more French verbs, I'll bet.'

Kieren looked up, startled. 'Oats! What are you doing here?' He knew at once it was a stupid question because Frazer was a fellow pupil. But he wasn't thinking clearly. He was also holding the letter. Too late, he tried to pocket it.

'Bet that's from my sister, isn't it?' Frazer declared, eyes gleaming. 'Well, that's family business so I'd like to read it, too.'

Even before the words were out of his mouth he'd darted forward, snatched the letter from Kieren's powerless fingers, spun round and dashed out of the room.

'Hey, that's mine!' Kieren wailed. 'Give it back, Oats!'

Of course, he knew Oats would do nothing of the sort. He'd seized a trophy and he was going to hang on to it. It was up to him to get it back before Oats had a chance to read it.

They were among the fastest players in the Rodale Goal Kings football team and so the chase was at a furious pace. 'Hey, watch it!' and 'Look where you're going!' were the most frequent and most polite complaints as they bounced off various shoulders and barged between pairs of chatting homeward-bound pupils. In recent times Frazer had developed a neat swerve to employ on the pitch against opponents. Here, he didn't have a ball at his feet and so his technique was practically faultless. Kieren, in spite of his desperate desire to recover his property, wasn't gaining on him. He knew it would be pointless to plead with the thief to stop; team-mates were always playing jokes on one another and rarely knew when to give up.

Suddenly, Frazer changed direction, turning sharply at right-angles to cut across the grassed area in front of the main building. He was aiming for a side entrance to the school grounds, often used by those who brought cycles and left them under cover by a gardening hut. If he'd managed to outrun Kieren then he might be able to pause and read the letter without being observed.

But he hadn't outrun him. When he glanced over his shoulder he saw that Kieren was still right behind him. So Frazer veered left, then right, then left again, ducking under the low branches of a cedar tree by the main gate before accelerating again in front of a dawdling group of year-12s, who broke into spontaneous jeering and yelled; 'Go for it, kid, go for it!' They hadn't a clue what he was doing, but they had to appear superior.

By now, Frazer was close to the junction with High Street, and it was at that point that Jane Allenby spotted him. She watched, fascinated, as he twisted and turned through the throng of pupils wending their way home. He was coming directly towards her and she halted, momentarily fearing that they'd collide head-on.

'Hello, Frazer,' she greeted him calmly. 'You're in a great hurry, aren't you? Nothing wrong, I hope.'

'Oh – oh – hi, Mrs Allenby! I – I –'

Now that he'd had to stop he couldn't prevent himself from turning round to see where Kieren was. And Kieren, too, had seen the Goal Kings' coach and was slowing down, though still determined to retrieve his precious letter. He didn't know whether Oats would really try to read every word of it, but he wasn't going to give him the chance.

'And Kieren, nice to see you, too,' Jane went on. 'But you look a bit flustered, to put it mildly. Everything all right?'

'No it isn't!' the captain of the Kings exploded. 'He's stolen something of mine and I want it back. *Now*!'

'What d'you mean' – Frazer was starting to say, when Kieren just lunged at him, grabbing the sheet of scented blue paper his team-mate was still holding in his right hand and promptly stuffing it out of sight in the inside pocket of his blazer. Frazer, caught off guard, stumbled and actually fell on his backside. Luckily for him, he landed on the grass verge and not on a paving stone.

Jane was startled. 'Boys, what's going on? Look, I can't have two of my players fighting each other, especially in public. What sort of image d'you think you're creating? People will think the Kings are a – a bunch of hooligans.'

She knew she was talking too much but she wanted to give them a chance to cool down. Because Dominic, her own son, was the same age she knew very well that passions among

5

teenage boys could run high (or, conversely, be hidden so deeply you'd never suspect they existed at all). She also knew that Kieren was friendly with Andrea, Frazer's sister, though why that could cause some sort of dispute between them she couldn't imagine. Unless, perhaps, Kieren had found another girlfriend and Frazer was trying to uphold the family's honour. Or maybe Frazer had found a girl-friend, one that Kieren also fancied. But no, she told herself, speculation like this was useless. Really, if relationships with girls was what it was all about, it was nothing to do with her.

'Well, unless this is something that directly affects the Goal Kings, all of us, then I suppose it's nothing to do with me what you're up to,' she admitted as Frazer McKinnon got to his feet and the two boys glared at each other. 'On the other hand, I don't want war breaking out among my players. Won't be much team spirit left among the Kings if two of you are knocking each other about. So I'd like to see the pair of you shake hands and tell me it won't happen again.'

Kieren knew there was nothing to be gained,

and quite a lot could be lost, by not following her request. After all, she'd appointed him as captain only recently and he was enjoying the role. Jane was always fair-minded in her treatment of players but she could be ruthless if necessary. Furthermore, he had got his letter back and Oats hadn't had a chance to read it.

'Sorry, Oats, sorry I knocked you down,' he said, holding out his hand and grinning. 'But don't forget you started it.'

Oats, too, was smiling as he returned a firm grip. 'Actually, I just slipped a wee bit, that's all. Was off balance.' He paused, his smile wider now, and then added: 'Anyway, I don't need to see your letter. I'll just ask Andi what's going on. She'll tell me, that's for sure.'

'She'd better not,' Kieren said warningly, though by now he was feeling happy that the letter was in his pocket.

'Well, now things are back to normal – more or less, anyway – I'll leave you to it.' As Jane was saying this, she saw Dominic approaching. And he was with a girl. Jane thought they were holding hands but couldn't be sure, because her son spotted her in the same instant and his fingers unlocked instantaneously.

'Oh, Mum, er, hi,' he greeted her nervously, his tongue flicking between his lips. 'Didn't expect to see you – or you guys, either,' he added, casting a despairing glance at his team-mates.

'Hi, you're Katie, aren't you?' Frazer said breezily, knowing very well who she was because she'd caught his eye at a Kings match. Her brother, Davey, was the team's leading scorer. He'd sensed that Dominic had no intention of introducing her. That, though, didn't surprise Frazer because he had an idea that Dominic wouldn't want any of the Kings to know about his friendship with her.

She just gave a slight nod and smiled at him in response. Clearly, she too was wishing this meeting wasn't taking place.

'I just happened to be passing on my way back from seeing a patient and thought you might like a lift home,' Jane explained. 'Nice to see you again, Katie. How's your mum? I was really pleased to see you both at the Scorton game. Hope you enjoyed it, even though we didn't manage to pull off a win.'

'Mum's fine, thanks, Mrs Allenby,' Katie answered. She kept glancing at Dominic to see how he was reacting to this tricky encounter but he was doing his best to avoid catching her eye.

For his part, Dominic was now exchanging glances with Kieren and Frazer who were grinning at him in united fashion as if they were amused by the fact that he'd been caught out in something he'd rather have kept secret.

'Do you think Davey's going to join us next?' Jane speculated aloud. 'If he does, we'll almost have enough players for a team meeting. Actually, we could do with one because there's plenty to discuss before the next match, against Wasperton.'

'Er, I think he's gone straight home, Mrs Allenby,' Katie offered. Any of her friends would have recognized her nervousness simply by her regular use of someone's name.

'Oh, well, I expect we'll all catch up with him later,' Jane went on blithely. She turned to her son. 'So, Dominic, would you like a lift? Oh, and Katie, too, if it's convenient?'

'Sorry, Mum, got something I – we, I mean – must do. Right, Katie?'

The dark-haired girl with attractive brown eyes momentarily looked surprised but then nodded eagerly. 'Sure, that's right.'

'So, see you, Mum,' murmured a relieved Dominic. 'Won't be in late. Oh, and thanks for offering a lift. Bye, you guys.'

And on that note the Kings' central defender defiantly took Katie's hand and steered her towards the lane that led to Candle Park. It immediately occurred to Jane that they certainly weren't heading for Katie Stroud's home, for that lay in practically the opposite direction. But then, Dominic hadn't said where they were going.

'So, what about you two?' Jane enquired. She was trying to be nonchalant, though she was still recovering from the realization that her only son had acquired a girlfriend, his first so far as she knew. She was aware that one or two of the boys in her squad were dating girls, though how strong those friendships were she had no idea. What worried her sometimes was the possibility that those relationships might become more important to them than their football. If that happened then there was the risk that the team's form might suffer.

'Oh, well, I'd like a lift, thanks, Coach,' Kieren replied. That would ensure that he didn't have to endure any more problems with Oats about the letter, now nestling safely in his pocket. He was even able to enjoy the new delay before he could read it.

'And me, too, thanks,' said Frazer. 'But you can drop me at Kieren's place, if you like. Easily walk from there.'

'Good! Right, let's get off. This will also give me a chance to mention something for the next game.'

As if to emphasize that he was the Kings' captain, and therefore should have preference in these matters, Kieren took the front passenger seat when they got into Mrs Allenby's car. First, though, she had to move her medical bag, which travelled everywhere with her in her job as a midwife.

'It might look as if you were a taxi driver if both of us sat in the back!' joked Kieren. That was also in the way of an apology to Oats for seizing the prime position.

'Oh, don't mind me, I like a wee bit more space when I can get it,' remarked Frazer, correctly interpreting Kieren's comment. While Kieren was tall and wiry, with surprisingly thin legs for such a fast player,

Frazer was built on much sturdier lines and, his parents forecast, would look much more like a rugby player when he finished growing.

Jane would have preferred to have had Frazer beside her because there was something she wanted to raise with him. Still, she would be able to gauge his reaction by glancing in her rear-view mirror; moreover, Kieren had to be involved, anyway, as the two of them were partners in defence.

'Frazer, I couldn't help seeing the way you were running this afternoon,' she began, neatly manoeuvring past a coal lorry (probably the only one still in existence in the entire Highlea district). 'The way you were nipping in between people and swerving so quickly. Very impressive.'

'Oh, really? Well, thanks, Mrs Allenby.' What on earth this was leading to he couldn't imagine, but he began to fear that it would end in some criticism of him. Surely she'd already said, more or less, that the incident with Kieren had nothing to do with her.

'Yes, and it made me think that we ought to make use of what you were doing because, almost every time you turned, it was to the left,' she went on. Frazer frowned because he couldn't see what difference that made to anything, but he remained silent.

'Now, you're normally a right-footed player in the centre of defence – but if we moved you a little further over to the left, well, that would ensure you could look after those opponents coming down their right wing or their inside-right channel,' she explained. 'You would reach them faster than someone whose first instinct is to move to the right. D'you see what I'm getting at?'

He did. But then, he was sure he'd known already that he usually defended in that way. Although he favoured his right foot he wasn't afraid of kicking with his left. Therefore the left side of defence seemed a natural place for him, especially as he liked to begin runs down that wing.

'Aye, I do,' he said cautiously. 'But d'you mean you want me to do things, well, differently?'

'No, no, Frazer, not at all,' she hastily reassured him. 'It's just that you can afford to play a little more towards the centre now, strengthen that area alongside Kieren. And

Kieren's left-footedness will mean that we're practically impregnable.'

'Well, *I* think that's a great idea, Coach,' Kieren chipped in. 'I mean, anything we do to keep the opposition out is bound to be good for us. Smart thinking, in my opinion.'

'Kieren, thank you!' she smiled. She hadn't expected such enthusiastic support from either of them. Of the two, she'd have preferred it to come from Frazer, but then he was more inclined to think before he spoke, in her experience. 'So, Frazer, will you be happy to keep a little closer to Kieren – oh, if you see what I mean!' she hurriedly added.

'Oh, aye,' he agreed, sounding as if he meant it. Kieren swung round in his seat to give his team-mate a wide smile and say: 'Well done, Oats. That's the spirit. Kings rule!'

That was the slogan favoured by most supporters of Rodale Goal Kings in the Highlea Sunday League, but it hadn't been heard much lately. After winning the Championship in dramatic fashion the previous season the team had made a calamitous start to the new season. Although there'd been some improvement in their fortunes, the Kings were still near the foot of the League table and their chances of retaining their title looked remote. Jane, however, hadn't given up hope and constantly was looking for ways to improve the team's performances and change their tactics where necessary. League regulations were fairly strict about signing new players in mid-season so she wasn't able to bring in anyone else to strengthen the squad unless there was an emergency of some kind, such as a particularly bad crop of injuries. So she had to make the most of the talents of the boys at present under her command.

It was while she was negotiating a tricky turning into the road where Kieren lived that her captain voiced a subject that she'd been turning over in her mind earlier that afternoon.

'Coach, are you thinking of bringing Danny back for the Wasperton game?' he wanted to know. 'I mean, I hope you don't mind me saying so, but Danny's our best goalkeeper by miles. Oh, and I know he feels really down at not playing for us regularly. That's right, isn't it, Oats?'

'Aye,' was the confirmation from the Scottish-born defender.

Jane slid the car into a vacant spot almost in front of Kieren's home, a manoeuvre that allowed her to give the impression she was concentrating on her driving rather than the question she'd been asked. She suspected there might be an ulterior motive behind it, something to do with Danny's off-the-pitch relationship with Kieren, but probably it would be best not to mention that, especially after the incident she'd witnessed outside the school between Kieren and Frazer.

'Well, I have thought about that,' she admitted after switching the engine off. 'I *do* know how Danny feels about it, Kieren. Know it probably better than anyone because he does talk to me. I also know how hard he's been training and how determined he is to win his place back. All the same, he did begin to lose concentration in matches. The mistakes he made were, well, rather painful for us, weren't they?'

She paused, though not because she was expecting an answer. Kieren, however, saw this as the ideal moment to stand up for his team-mate. 'Yeah, but you know Danny, Coach. He doesn't go on worrying if something's gone

16

wrong, he just makes sure he's not at fault again. Oh, yeah, and you can't tell if he's got over his mistakes if you don't try him in goal again, can you?'

'That's very shrewd of you, Kieren,' she replied approvingly. 'But tell me this, don't you think Harry Greenland's a good replacement? He made some terrific saves in our last match. Kept us in the game at least twice.'

'Yeah, that's right,' Kieren conceded. 'But, well, I think the rest of the defence has a better understanding with Danny.'

'Really? Because one of the things I had to tell him not so long ago was that he ought to communicate more. Tell you when he was coming for the ball, claim it when it was definitely his. Of course, that applies to the rest of you, too. Frazer, what's your opinion?'

'Oh, Icy's OK, I suppose,' was the casual answer. As everyone seemed to like to call him Oats because of his Scottish origin he enjoyed using others' nicknames, and Icy was an obvious choice for someone called Harry Greenland. 'But maybe Danny's the better goalie – most of the time!'

It was in Jane's mind that Kieren might be

making this plea on behalf of Danny because he'd succeeded him as team captain. It was she who'd made the change when she dropped Danny, because she couldn't have a skipper who wasn't in the team. Moreover, Kieren had been outstanding during the Championship season and she knew he was in the selectors' minds for a trial with the county team.

'Well, it's good to see how loyal you are to each other,' she remarked, turning to smile at Frazer. 'So I'll –'

'What does Dom think?' Kieren interrupted her. 'I mean, he's just as much a central defender as me and Oats.'

'Kieren, you know I have a rule that I don't discuss team matters at home with Dominic,' she chided him. 'And Dominic doesn't carry tales from the dressing-room. That's the only way it can work if I'm to be completely fair as a coach.'

'Oh, yeah, I suppose so,' replied Kieren, not sounding convinced. As, indeed, he wasn't; he couldn't believe that the topic of the Goal Kings was banned in a household which included a player as well as a coach. It was bad enough at *his* home, for his mum, Jakki, was one of the Kings' most enthusiastic supporters and she wanted to know every little thing about team affairs. She was constantly badgering him for news. He didn't really mind because she was as keen as he was to see his football career blossom.

Almost as if she'd read his thoughts, Jane Allenby glanced across at his house as if checking to see whether Jakki Kelly was about. She was rather hoping she wasn't, because sometimes Kieren's mum had *too* much to say about the Kings and their position in the League table. At present she would be entitled to ask just what Jane was going to do to propel them higher. The straight answer was that she wasn't entirely sure, but she had some positive ideas which she'd rather keep to herself for the present.

'Well, give my best wishes to your mum and tell her I'll see her on Sunday,' she told Kieren as he got out of the car and thanked her for the lift. Before she could invite Frazer to stay in for the short trip to his house he, too, speedily slid out. Both paused politely to wave goodbye as she headed down the avenue.

'You know what, I'll bet old Jane thinks you

asked about Danny because you're feeling guilty at pinching the captaincy off him,' Frazer commented as they stood together on the pavement. 'But –'

'I *didn't* pinch it,' Kieren protested hotly. 'I was given it. Didn't even know it was happening until she rang me to say she wanted me to have the job. Couldn't refuse it, could I? Somebody's got to be skipper and I'm as good as anybody in the team and better than most.'

Frazer patiently waited for him to finish before saying: 'When you interrupted me I was about to say that *I* know that you're feeling guilty about something else – about pinching Danny's girlfriend off him!'

Now Kieren really felt like exploding. 'I did not! Danny was never her real boyfriend. He never got anywhere with her. She told me that. I'm the one that she wants, Oats! That's why she sends me lo – letters.'

'Oh, sure, I believe every word of that,' Frazer said airily. 'That's why I'm going home now to see Andi and find out all that's going on. See you, KK.'

'See you, Oats,' Kieren responded, remaining on the pavement for a few moments to watch him leave. This time he'd not thought of running after him.

As he opened the front door his mum was waiting for him.

'I saw that Jane brought you and Frazer home so you must have been discussing the Goal Kings,' she greeted him. 'So, come on, tell me what ideas she's got for the next match. She's got to do something drastic to get us up that League table. Is she going to make some changes in the team?'

Her tall, gangly son shrugged; 'Search me Mum. She didn't tell us anything. But she listened to our ideas, mine and Oats'. She said she'll definitely take them into her plans before she decides on anything.'

'Oh, did she?' remarked Jakki Kelly, running her fingers through her short blonde hair and looking astonished. 'She did, did she?'

2 *Warnings*

Jane felt she could begin to relax just a little when the Kings' second goal went in. It had been scored with his customary clinical efficiency by Davey Stroud, finishing off a powerful run and cross from his co-striker, Josh Rowley.

Their opponents, Wasperton, were new-comers to the Highlea Junior Sunday League and naturally wanted to make an impact against Rodale Goal Kings, the current Champions. They'd very nearly succeeded in dramatic fashion. Harry Greenland, the Kings' improving goalkeeper, was forced to tip a thunderous drive over the bar in the first moments of the game. Then, barely two minutes later, he was diving full-length to turn away another powerful shot at the expense of giving away a corner. Those two near misses, however, seemed to take some of the sting from the Wasps, as they were popularly known (and, just as predictably, their colours were yellow-and-black with black shorts, in contrast to the Kings' purple-and-white shirts and white shorts).

Then, when the Kings scored the first goal of the game, it was a body blow for the Wasps because they practically presented it to the Kings on a plate. Reuben Jones, the Kings' inventive midfielder with a talented left foot, chipped an exquisite pass to Davey Stroud on the edge of the box. Davey trapped the ball instantaneously, swivelled, swung his left foot and hit a scorching shot at goal. To his credit, the goalie got his hands to it but couldn't hold on to the ball. As it spilled from his arms the predatory Josh Rowley reached it first to stab it into the net from the closest range.

Five minutes later those roles were reversed when Davey converted Josh's cross for the home side to double their lead; and Jane's worries began to recede.

'Kings rule! Kings rule!' some of their supporters began to chant, although the crowd was smaller than had become customary last season.

Even though it did begin to look as though her players were regaining their confidence, and were therefore beginning to fashion goal-scoring opportunities whenever they attacked, Jane felt it was premature to start singing their own special anthem. That run of defeats and snatched draws earlier in the season meant that the Kings still had mountains to climb. Even if they did collect three points today they'd still be hovering only just above a relegation position. No, it definitely wasn't a time to sound triumphant. 'Things are looking up at last, don't you think?' murmured a voice in Jane's ear. She turned to smile at Jakki Kelly!, who could usually be relied upon to state the obvious, or almost the obvious. 'The boys are showing the sort of form that won us the Championship,' continued Kieren's mum.

'Don't know that I'd go as far as that, Jakki,' replied the coach. 'I think there's work to do yet to get them playing with the kind of rhythm and purpose they showed at the end of last season. Maybe when we've won – what? – five games on the bounce, then I'll agree with you.'

'Jane, you're getting to be a real pessimist!'

Jakki grinned. 'Honestly, that's no good in a coach. You've got to set an example and *glow* with optimism – and determination. That's what the boys need. Then you'll see a real difference in them.'

'Oh, I'm sure nobody would argue with that,' replied Jane smoothly, because there was no point in saying anything else. In spite of knowing her for some years she still wasn't sure she really understood what motivated Jakki Kelly. On the surface, Jakki was always supportive of the team and friendly to Jane; from time to time she'd given hints that she'd like to have a stronger role in the life of the Goal Kings and Jane suspected that the blonde former rock singer would like to take her place as coach. But was that because she genuinely believed she could help all of them to achieve more success; or would it simply be the easiest way of promoting the prospects of her only son, Kieren, captain of the Kings?

Those thoughts were a distraction, as Jane realized when, suddenly, she saw that the Kings had conceded a free kick just on the edge of their own penalty area. There weren't many players of this age who could score direct from that distance, but you could never rule it out; and Wasperton were a team of unknown skills as far as she was concerned. The kick had been awarded because of a mistimed and over-fierce tackle and Jane was surprised to see that the culprit was Lloyd Colmer. Normally, Lloyd played as a creative midfielder, for he could pass well and produce some excellent attacking runs; he didn't play the ball-winning hard man.

Now he was hanging his head as he listened to a stern reprimand from the balding referee. Jane wondered what had provoked him to act as he did, for it was out of character. On the other hand, she had recently felt the need to tell him to sharpen up his game, for his form wasn't as good as last season's. So perhaps he was trying to show her that his tackling was improving.

Fortunately, the ref didn't deem the offence worthy of a yellow card and when the lecture was over Lloyd glanced towards the touchline as if to check whether his coach too was angry with him. His focus, though, seemed to be a little further along the touchline and Jane assumed that Lloyd's mum was present as usual. However, there was no sign of Serena Colmer. Usually the flamboyant colours of her skirts made her impossible to miss but today the brightest attire was Jakki's red-and-yellow waterproof.

It was an inventive free kick. Instead of hammering it into the Kings' defensive wall, or trying to float the ball over it, the kicker directed it to the team-mate positioned at the very end of the wall. He moved barely half a metre before backheeling it strongly into the heart of the box – and behind the slowly disintegrating wall. The sharpest mover among the Wasps was on to it before any home defender. All the attacker needed to do then was to flick it sideways beyond the onrushing keeper.

The sight of Harry Greenland flinging himself bodily towards him was enough to make the striker gasp – and his chance of glory had gone. Harry smothered the ball as if he were trapping a rodent.

'Saved, Harry!' his coach yelled in appreciation. She'd been certain the Wasps would score.

'Great save, Harry!' Jakki echoed.

Danny, standing close to them, said nothing at all. That so surprised Jane that she turned to see what he was doing. And Danny appeared to be staring at Katie Stroud, a little further along the touchline. Quite often Danny gave vocal encouragement to Harry, his successor as the Kings' goalkeeper, something that Jane admired. She'd had to replace Danny both as skipper and keeper earlier in the season but Danny had shown no resentment. Indeed, he'd displayed an admirable sense of team spirit by continuing to support his team-mates, all of them, in every way he could. Jane thought that one day he'd make an exceptional diplomat.

She knew that Katie was there to support the team (she'd cheered loudly to mark her brother's goal) but doubtless her chief interest was in Dominic. So far, Jane's son had said very little about his new friendship and she wasn't going to risk embarrassing him by asking anything. No doubt in time he'd tell her something. If the relationship with Katie continued.

Again, her attention to the game was alerted by another scything tackle from Lloyd. It occurred on the left wing, only a few metres from where she was standing. To reach the boy on the ball the Kings' midfielder had sprinted past Frazer, almost elbowing him out of the way. The Wasperton player was hit so hard he tumbled over the touchline. He got up so angrily that it was plain he wasn't hurt. But the ref took action before the victim had a chance to wreak his own vengeance. The yellow card was being flourished even before he spoke a word.

'You're very lucky this isn't a red – you practically deserve that,' was what he said so loudly that every spectator must have heard it. 'Do anything, anything at all, like that again and you'll spend the rest of this match in the changing-room.'

Once again Lloyd looked ashamed of himself but he still was casting glances along the touchline. Jane, following his glances, saw a stranger, a stocky man wearing a black woollen coat. Jane had never seen him before, but it could easily be Lloyd's father. If so, was it his presence here today that explained Serena's absence?

The booking wasn't the worst outcome of

Lloyd's offence. Once again, Wasperton showed real imagination in the manner of taking the free kick. The ball was hit as hard as possible crossfield to their loping full-back – and he accelerated to take the ball in his stride and keep running. Kings were slow to spot the danger. Kieren was sprinting back towards his own penalty area but Dominic, for once, was slow to move. Harry, guessing what was coming, edged from his line, yelling for some cover. There was time for it to arrive but it didn't; well, not enough of it.

The raiding full-back cleverly rounded Matthew Forrest, the Kings' right-sided defender, looked up and then very astutely pulled the ball back into the path of Wasperton's main striker, who was arriving on the edge of the box at great speed. Moments before he'd been loitering on the far flank, acting as a sort of decoy, and no one had moved to mark him. Now, as the ball reached him, he made no effort to take it under his control. Instead, he hit it on the half-volley before anyone could attempt a tackle. His aim could not have been better, the power he produced was exceptional and so the ball flew bullet-like beyond Harry's reach and into the top corner of the net. By any standards, it was a wonderful and spectacular goal.

Deservedly, the scorer was swamped by his ecstatic team-mates. 'I'll never score another goal as good as that!' he exclaimed at the top of his voice. 'You'd better – that's what you're in the team for,' responded his demanding coach.

'He should never have got near that ball,' complained Kieren, though he stopped short of levelling blame at any one of his team-mates. In part, that was because he felt himself to be at fault. So far he hadn't said a word to Lloyd about his part in the events leading up to the goal but he would do at half-time, which was due shortly. Meanwhile, he was urging the Kings to regain their two-goal lead against a team he felt they should beat easily.

Somehow, though, that third goal wouldn't come. Twice Reuben Jones created chances almost from nothing but Josh Rowley squandered the first when he tried a first-time shot before he had control of the ball, and then Lloyd, rushing to join an attack to make amends for his errors in defence, hit his shot so wide of the goal that it was nearer to striking a corner flag.

Naturally, Jane was unhappy with the Kings' performance when she confronted them at the interval. 'I don't know what's got into you since you scored the second goal. Everything's gone to pieces. Maybe you're just trying too hard, though it doesn't look like that. Lloyd, do you think a war's broken out? You look as though you're trying to put opponents in hospital, the way you're tackling them. You've already got one yellow card – deservedly, in my view – and if you get another then the whole team will suffer because we'll be down to ten men.'

She paused to give him a chance to explain what he was up to, but he simply mumbled: 'Sorry, coach.'

'I didn't see your mum among the spectators today,' Jane continued, rather more cautiously. 'Is she OK?'

There was a moment's hesitation before Lloyd said quietly: 'My dad's here today. He and Mum have split. She says she doesn't want to be anywhere near him. Dad said he wanted to see me play today.'

'Oh,' said Jane, knowing how inadequate that response was. But what could she say that would help? 'Lloyd, I'm sorry that things are bad at home for you. Wish I could do something to help but I don't suppose I can. Look, would you rather miss the second half? I could –'

'Oh, no, Mrs Allenby,' he cut in. 'I want to show Dad that I'm going to be a top player. I *need* to. Please.'

Jane was wishing she'd never started this conversation with Lloyd. It was impossible to make promises to him about what she'd do; and she knew that if he committed another offence the ref would be forced to discipline him. And that would penalize the entire team. She saw that his team-mates were taking an interest in the conversation and she didn't want to risk embarrassing him by continuing it.

'OK, we'll leave things as they are, Lloyd, but take care – and don't make any more rash tackles.'

'Look, I think I was to blame for their goal,' Kieren cut in quickly. 'I mean, I was supposed to be marking their number 10, but I sort of let him drift out of sight. Sorry, Coach, It won't happen again.'

'Kieren, I like your honesty,' his coach smiled at him. 'And you're absolutely right. Our concentration has begun to wander a bit. But that applies to several of you – no point in naming names, you know who I mean. If you'd all been concentrating then we'd have prevented their goal.'

She paused, then added: 'I've always thought that 2–0 is a dangerous score. Teams with that lead often sit back on it, thinking they've probably done enough to win the match. Then if they concede one goal they can panic and start defending rather desperately. All too many times they then concede an equalizer – and after that the game's up for grabs, if that's the correct expression nowadays.'

Nobody told her it wasn't. She'd heard Dominic use it and, instinctively, she glanced at him. At that moment he was looking elsewhere and she thought it was at Katie, now directly opposite her and the Kings on the far touchline.

'So, *all* of you,' she said emphatically, 'don't

let your concentration lapse again. I don't want any panic setting in. Wasperton are a decent side but they aren't as good as us. So I expect us to beat them today and collect three points. Remember, Kings, we need 'em!'

As the teams returned for the second half Dominic sprinted across the pitch for a few words with Katie, watched not only by his mum but by Danny, though the expression on Danny's face was giving nothing away about his feelings. He was still hoping that he'd be called on soon to replace Harry in goal and yet, as each match was played, it was clear that Harry was still improving as a keeper. Already Danny was beginning to wonder how long he could wait before looking for another team in another league. His loyalty to the Kings wouldn't last for ever.

When they'd won the toss, Wasperton had chosen which end to attack rather than to kick off. This meant that the Kings were now playing towards the cricket-pavilion end, which they normally chose to do in the first half when they won the toss, and Jane couldn't help wondering whether this would make any difference to them. Unwisely, she mentioned this to Jakki, who had glided up to stand beside her again.

'Honestly, Jane, you're not only a pessimist, you're a superstitious pessimist!' Jakki laughed, although she couldn't conceal a hint that she was also being serious. 'Surely the direction of the play doesn't matter a jot.'

'Well, you might think so, but football is absolutely riddled with superstitions. Players who put on the left sock first, or always have to be last to leave the dressing-room – things like that. Every player is familiar with those sort of rituals. So are other sports, too. There was that racehorse trainer who always had to wear a red shirt at the races – and, oh yes, an England football manager who never changed his suit during the season in case he changed the team's luck. Dominic could list scores of examples, I'm sure. He's hot on facts like those.'

Jakki shrugged. 'Well, if that's what switches you on then I suppose others have to live with it. Don't think Kieren even knows what the word superstition means!'

Before Jane could say another word on the matter another explosive moment on the pitch took all her attention. The referee was backing away from a posse of players seemingly intent on pursuing him in the Kings' penalty area. And all of them were wearing purple-and-white shirts.

'What happened?' Jane gasped.

'Search me,' replied an equally baffled Jakki.

'Dom handled the ball,' Danny supplied. 'Couldn't get out of it. Sheer bad luck. But the ref's obviously going to award a penalty. They're all the same; never take any notice of anyone who really saw what happened.'

Jane was worried that the kind of protests her players were making would lead to a rash of yellow cards for them; and these days the guilty ones could be banned for several matches if they collected more than one card. With a small squad such as the Kings possessed the loss of any player was a major setback.

Thankfully, the ref merely waved the protesters away and then indicated that the Wasperton player should take his kick. The striker went about it with all the ease of an experienced professional, slotting it just inside the right-hand post so that even a goalkeeper diving full-length wouldn't have got to it. Harry waited until the last split second before moving, but had no earthly chance of saving the shot.

'Oh, no!' murmured Jane, 'I warned them about that 2–0 lead – and now it's gone.'

Jakki hadn't heard the coach's interval remarks about the dangerous score; had she done so then doubtless she'd have regarded it as another empty superstition. 'Rotten luck, just when we were doing so well,' was all she could say. 'Now we'll need Kieren to gee them up a bit, get them back in front.'

Jane thought that was her job but, with play naturally continuing, there wasn't much she could do about it until she could get a word to her players. They had resumed on the attack and Reuben neatly foxed two opponents on a mazy run before he was brought down with a bulldozing tackle. His coach thought that merited a yellow card but it didn't bring one.

Unfortunately, the Kings weren't able to profit from the kick and moments later the attacking Wasps were swarming into their opponents' half with every intention of getting three points out of this match. Soon, every home player with the exception of Davey Stroud had dropped back to help their beleaguered defence; now that they'd given up the midfield it meant they hardly had a chance of winning the match themselves. Despairingly, Jane tried to signal to Kieren in order to pass on new instructions. But he never looked in her direction. Now all she could do was make a substitution or hope that someone would need medical attention so that a message could be relayed while she was tending to the injured player.

Then Lloyd had another rush of blood to the head. For some time he'd been involved in a running battle with a Wasperton midfielder and the scuffles for possession were getting fiercer. It was impossible to see who was really to blame when both boys crashed to the ground in a tangle of limbs. Jane saw that Lloyd kicked out at his opponent as he scrambled to his feet and she thought that it might be in retaliation because Lloyd then began hopping about, clutching his ankle as if it had been hurt. The referee might well have been looking in another direction when the incident started but he caught up with it as

Lloyd continued to complain and yell at his adversary, who was now rubbing the inside of his thigh as if he, too, had suffered in the collision.

'Oh, no, don't send him off!' Jane pleaded silently as the ref launched into a lecture on the penalties for bad behaviour. Lloyd was good at looking contrite but on this occasion he was plainly ready to defend himself and condemn his opponent. The ref would have none of that. The clash was near enough for Jane to hear the summing up: 'You've already got one card, son, and you're within a millimetre of getting another – and that means the end of the game for you. Think about that. Don't go on being stupid. The pair of you – behave – or else . . .'

He was leaving his warning hanging in the air and turning away when Jane managed to attract his attention. He saw that she wanted to make a substitution and nodded his approval when she indicated that Lloyd was the player she was taking off. It was a decision that ought to make control of the match a little easier for him. Hastily, she told Sean Ferriby that he was taking Lloyd's place.

'Sean, go and do your best by running with the ball – go at them,' she instructed him. 'Tell Kieren from me we've got to get out of our own penalty area. We're defending far too deep. We're just surrendering three-quarters of the pitch to them.'

He nodded and dashed to the far side of the pitch to take up his position and pass on her words to his skipper, who had seized his chance to have a word with Andrea. Jane hadn't noticed her arrival but she frowned at what was going on. Kieren shouldn't be chatting to spectators at a time like this; his concentration on the match should be total. It occurred to her to mention this to Jakki. But before she could open her mouth she thought again. No, that would be quite unfair: it was her job to speak to a player about his conduct on the pitch, not the player's mum's.

Because of all that had been happening on the pitch it was a minute or so before she remembered Lloyd and the need to have a word with him about his substitution. It was always her practice to explain to a player exactly why she'd taken him off and thank him for his contribution to the game. She was well aware how much some boys resented being replaced and then feared that they'd also be excluded for the next match.

She looked along the touchline but there was no sign of Lloyd. Surprised, she turned round and then spotted Lloyd walking away towards the car park beside the man in the black coat, who had his arm round the boy's shoulder.

Jane was in a quandary. She needed to say something to him about the substitution yet she couldn't really turn her back on the match, not even for half a minute. Again, she thought of Jakki, but couldn't ask her to do her job for her.

'Lloyd! Don't go! I want a word,' she called.

The pair of them halted and then swung round to face her as she hurried towards them. 'Look, I'm sorry I had to take you off, Lloyd, but it seemed the sensible thing – didn't want you *sent* off.'

'Listen, lady, I'm not having my son treated like that by anybody,' the man answered. He had a deep voice but didn't raise it; he was just matter-of-fact rather than angry. 'I am taking him to his proper home. He will be happy there.'

'But Dad, this is –' Lloyd started to say when his father interrupted.

'This is not the time to talk, son. This is the right time to walk away. I have nothing more to say.'

With that he gently steered Lloyd back on the route to the car park. Jane sensed there was no point in trying to discuss anything with the man. He had made up his mind what he was going to do and would brook no argument. Lloyd's expression was a mixture of embarrassment and dejection and Jane wished she'd been able to offer him some comforting words about the future. Although his form had been very mixed recently that was almost certainly because of tensions in his home life. Once those problems were over she was sure he'd recover his exuberance and his determination to do everything he could for his beloved Kings. Well, she could only hope that time would sort things out for Lloyd.

'What was all that about?' enquired Jakki.

'Tell you later,' was Jane's reply. No doubt before she did so Jakki would have quizzed Kieren, who might well know a good deal more about Lloyd's family problems than she did.

Sean was involved in the action almost immediately, hunting down a loose ball following one of Harry's long clearances and then cleverly feeding Reuben with a reverse pass. The skill of that manoeuvre surprised Jane. Since adding him to her squad at the start of the season after he'd been released by his former club, Greendown, Sean had often looked very ordinary both in training and in matches, which was why he hadn't been her first choice for a midfield role. But perhaps he was still coming to terms with joining a team that were the current Champions and therefore filled with players who had already proved themselves winners.

Reuben very cleverly made progress and then managed to hold on to the ball when challenged. One of his attributes was that, in spite of his almost fragile frame, he was hard to knock off the ball. He was awaiting the ideal moment to hit a pass to Davey, now racing forward at top speed from a deep defensive position. Sean moved out left, calling for the ball, but in reality acting as a decoy. When he drew two defenders to him a gap opened up on the right. Davey, taking the ball in his stride, was through in a flash and surprised everyone by the timing of his shot on goal. He hit it almost immediately.

The Wasps' goalie was only fractionally off his line but even if he'd been behind it probably he'd never have got to Davey's shot, hit with venom and accuracy. Except that it wasn't quite accurate enough. It struck the base of the right-hand post and then rebounded so far that a defender outside the penalty area was the one to collect it and clear it.

Davey flung his hands up to his head and arched his back in despair at not getting the reward he felt he deserved, that the Kings deserved. Lefty had supplied a dream of a pass and it ought to have led to a winning goal.

Still, it cheered up the home spectators. Led by his sister, Katie, and Andrea, the cries rang out: 'Kings rule! Kings rule!' Jakki, too, was applauding vigorously and Jane was shouting: 'Well done, Sean. Well done, Davey! Keep it up, boys. Come on, come on!'

Sean was thrilled to hear his name being sung out. He'd long felt that probably Mrs Allenby didn't rate him, mainly because

Dominic had criticized his first touch in an early training session. And he imagined that Dominic and his mum would be bound to discuss team matters and individual players when they were in their own home together. Harry Greenland, who'd joined the Kings at the same time as himself, had tried to assure him that the coach didn't do anything of the kind but Sean found that impossible to accept. Now, though, she was plainly pleased with him. Maybe she liked players who weren't physically very big but who could run and turn and shoot; after all, those were Davey's characteristics and it was widely believed among the squad that he was Coach Allenby's favourite player (and he had been given the Player-of-the-Season Award following their success in the Championship).

Within a couple of minutes he was sure things were looking up for him when he received a precise pass from Dominic, of all people, and the accompanying yell: 'Go for it, Sean!'

He went for it. Darting one way and then another, his close control as good as it had ever been, the Kings' substitute weaved his way through a thicket of defenders just inside the Wasps' half. He was aware of Josh Rowley pounding down the right flank and signalling with an arm above his head that he was ready for a pass. Sean ignored him and spun in the opposite direction. Davey, too, wanted the ball but Sean intended to make further progress before giving the ball to anyone. Just to his right was Reuben, always so easily identified by his floating, flaxen hair. Reuben would be his target after he'd got past one more opponent.

Again he jinked to his left before turning right to go past that opponent – and he would have outwitted him but for a moment of sheer bad luck. The ball flicked up from a divot, Sean slowed to regain control of it and his opponent pounced, throwing himself into the Kings' player from behind. Sean went down in a heap, pain searing through him as the other boy's studs scraped down his thigh.

'Sorry, mate, didn't mean to get you like that,' the boy apologized, holding out his hand to try to haul Sean to his feet. Sean was in neither the mood nor the position to accept it. His hands were clutching his leg, trying to do something to stem the pain.

'Totally unacceptable, that was!' thundered the ref, scrabbling in his pocket for a red card. 'I've already warned you about violent tackles of that kind. Well, you wouldn't listen so now you're off. Go on, get off the pitch. You might have done untold damage here.'

Jane Allenby was already trying to discover the extent of it. She had to part Sean's hands to get to the wound and start to clean it up. Her medical training convinced her that stitches wouldn't be necessary, but the wound needed covering. Sean's sobs had eased and he tried to move.

'Just keep still a little longer, Sean,' his coach said gently. 'I know it must hurt a lot but I'll give you something to take that away.'

'My mum won't see it, will she?' the Kings' substitute asked anxiously.

'Well, it's a bit high up on your leg for that, even if you're wearing shorts,' she replied, trying to keep her surprise out of her voice. 'Is there, er, a problem with your mum?'

'She sort of panics if me or Patrick – he's my brother – gets a knock,' was the answer. 'She says that soccer's too rough.'

'I'll have a word with her, if you like, tell her what's happened,' Jane volunteered.

'No, no, don't do that!' Sean pleaded. 'That'd make things worse. Don't tell her *anything*.'

'Listen, we've got to get you off the pitch, Sean. I'm putting Gareth on in your place,' she explained. 'We can't take any risks with an injury like yours. I'm sure it'll clear up in a couple of days. Meanwhile, you've just got to take things easy.'

He didn't argue. Although the pain was easing he couldn't move without it affecting him. By now the game was in progress again and his attacker was out of sight, escorted to a car in the car park by a Wasperton supporter. Glumly he watched Gareth Kingstree make a complete hash of the first pass he received after taking Sean's place.

The Kings weren't able to exploit any gaps left by the player sent off and, as the game moved into its final minutes, Wasperton were looking the stronger side.

'Come on, you Kings, don't let 'em get away with a point!' yelled Jakki. She thought all the home supporters should be providing vocal encouragement, but most were watching in complete silence.

Jane shot her a grateful glance, feeling a little guilty that she herself was saying nothing. Could she do anything more to shake up the attack so that Davey and Josh could somehow get the winner? To her own dismay, she couldn't think of anything. For some reason her players simply weren't functioning as a team. Somehow, too, the fates seemed to be against them. Almost as soon as Sean had come on and provided instant inspiration with his clever dribbling, changes of pace and shrewd passing he was literally knocked out of the game. She glanced at him now. She'd made sure he put on his tracksuit to keep warm but he hadn't wanted to retreat to the dressing-room. Looking paler than usual he was standing on the touchline, arms folded, thinking about his future in the team. He was well aware that injured players who missed matches could so easily lose their place for a long time, for it had happened to him with his previous club, Greendown.

Then, with the referee already having looked at his watch once, Wasperton threw themselves into what they knew might be their final attack. Once again they found the Kings' defence retreating, back-pedalling rather than trying to tackle anyone. The Wasps' number 10 was lucky with a rebound from someone's ankle when he tried to thread a pass into the box. This time he turned with the ball, taking Kieren with him; but then, totally unexpectedly, he repeated his favourite trick: with lots of force, he back-heeled the ball into the middle. It went past Dominic before he even saw it and so there was no one to challenge Wasperton's other striker.

He swooped on the ball by the penalty spot, switched it from one foot to the other as he spotted a gap and then very neatly indeed flicked it into the net well beyond Harry Greenland's stretching left hand.

Rodale Goal Kings 2, Wasperton 3.

'Oh *no*!' wailed Jane and Jakki simultaneously.

Sean Ferriby dropped his head into his hands. The pain of a home defeat was almost as bad as that caused by his injury. He really believed he was going to establish himself in the side in this match and now, well, he was in no-man's-land.

All Jane's fears about teams relaxing after leading 2–0 had come home to roost. It was uncanny. It was almost as if the Champions were determined to throw away the title they'd worked so hard to win the previous season. What was even worse, if possible, was that they'd gone down to a team reduced to ten men, and the winning goal had been scored after that dismissal. It was the lowest point in her relationship with Rodale Goal Kings JFC, a relationship that had touched the stratosphere only a few months earlier when the Championship Trophy had been won so gloriously.

'It's just, well, unbelievable, isn't it?' murmured Jakki, returning to stand beside the stricken coach. 'How're we going to get over this?'

'I wish I knew, Jakki, I really wish I knew,' was all Jane could say.

3 A Game for a Girl?

Danny Loxham was flicking through the TV channels with the sort of aimlessness that soon began to irritate his dad. David Loxham was working at the table on the other side of the sitting-room, trying to make sense of some sales figures supplied by one of his colleagues. They literally didn't add up.

'Danny, for goodness' sake, give it a rest,' he pleaded eventually. 'What's got into you? You look as if you're bored out of your mind.'

'I am.'

Mr Loxham put down his pen, looking thoroughly surprised. 'That's not like you, Dan. Are you sure you're feeling OK?'

'Yeah, I'm fine. Just bored. Nothing's going right for me. Not the boxing, not the football, not gi – nothing.'

His father would have been happy to talk things through with him if he hadn't needed to finish his paperwork as soon as possible in order to watch a favourite programme later in the evening. Because there were only the two of them now, Danny's mother having left home more than a year ago, he had the responsibilities of both parents; moreover, he always put his son first in his life.

'Listen, Dan, we can talk later – I promise I will – so why don't you go and phone a friend or something? What about that Scottish boy – Frazer, isn't it? – who also plays for the Kings?'

'No way! Not ringing him.' He couldn't explain that he wouldn't quite know what to say if Andrea, Frazer's sister, answered the phone. For she had dumped him in favour of Kieren. He didn't bear Kieren any grudges but at present he couldn't cope with Andrea.

'Well, then, somebody else,' his dad urged. 'Go on. I'll finish sooner if you do.'

'OK.' He got up and collected the mobile phone from the entrance hall before going up to his room. Ringing somebody wasn't a bad idea because if he could get hold of the right person then there was a lot to talk about. Since the defeat by Wasperton he'd been brooding about the Kings and his future with them. Or was it his lack of any future with them? Danny was beginning to think it looked that way, for Mrs Allenby seemed too preoccupied to chat to him about anything at all to do with the team. Yet, only a few weeks ago, he'd been captain of the team as well as first-choice goalkeeper. He knew his form had dipped after he'd suffered a rib injury in training but nowadays he'd never been fitter (his boxing training alone saw to that). Trouble was, Harry Greenland's form in goal was getting better all the time. So Jane Allenby had no reason to drop him. Icy Greenland, it had to be admitted, was just about the only King really playing at the top of his game.

Mentally, Danny ran through the list of team-mates he wouldn't mind talking to, having discarded other friends and school-mates. Kieren? No; KK, would, at this time in the evening, almost certainly be with Andrea at his place or hers. Dominic? Hardly, because his mum might answer the phone and it wouldn't be the best way of talking to Mrs Allenby.

Thoughts of Dominic reminded him of Katie Stroud, Davey's sister. Danny had heard that

Dominic was dating Katie, a girl who'd already caught Danny's eye when she was present at a Kings' match earlier in the season. At that time he still had hopes of his relationship with Andrea, so he'd merely kept her in mind for a future date. It hadn't occurred to him that Dominic would make a move in her direction because the Kings' central defender hadn't previously expressed any interest in girls.

Now he pondered whether to ring her brother while hoping that she would answer the phone; for if she did so he could chat with her and test her mood and her attitude to him; if Davey answered then they could talk about football for a bit before he made some casual inquiries about Katie. Yes, that would work very well, whatever happened.

What Danny hadn't anticipated was that no one would answer; the Stroud family, it appeared, were all out. Well, he knew his luck was out, so that should have been predictable. Frowning, he glanced down the list of the rest of his team-mates. And he couldn't see one name he wanted to ring.

He leaned back, his grey eyes gazing at the

image of himself in the mirror, wishing that he could think of something that would cheer him up.

Kieren and Andrea had been talking in her room for some time when, without warning, she changed the subject completely. 'Listen, KK, what do you think of girls playing footie? Playing for real, I mean, not just hoofing a ball around on the touchline because they're bored?'

'Haven't really thought about it,' he answered. 'Suppose it's all right. But, well, if it was you playing I'd be worried you might get injured.'

'No, you wouldn't. I don't keep on worrying about you getting injured when I'm watching you. All players of both sexes get knocks. It's part of the game. You haven't got to worry about it in advance.'

'OK, I agree,' he smiled. 'So what're you on about?'

'Playing for the Kings. Me. A girl. Playing in the same team as you. Soon. That's what I'm on about. Want to know what you, my very best friend in all the world, thinks about *that*.'

If any other girl had asked him that he'd have laughed. But it was plain that Andrea McKinnon really was wanting his opinion on a subject that meant a great deal to her. He already knew that she enjoyed training sessions in their garden with her brother Frazer and that she generally loved the game. What he hadn't known about was her ambition to be a player.

'Well, I don't really know what to say, Andi,' he replied cautiously. 'I mean, I don't think there's any chance. I don't think Jane Allenby would pick a girl, for a start. We haven't got one in the squad and I don't know that we could sign anybody else.'

Andrea tossed her pony-tail smartly from one side to the other and back again, a sign that she wasn't pleased with what she was hearing. 'Kieren, that's just a technical detail. I'm not talking about that sort of thing. I want to know what you think about *me* being in the team.'

'Well, *I* think it'd be a great idea because I'd get to see more of you – well, I can't really see any more, can I?' he grinned. 'But I'd be dead jealous if other guys saw you as well when we're in the dressing-room!'

'Oh, Kieren, I'm not talking about that side of it,' she said with some exasperation. 'None of that's important and it certainly won't bother me if I have to change in a room full of boys – and it shouldn't bother them. I just want to be a player, not a "girl-player". The thing that matters is, d'you think the coach will go for it if I prove I'm good enough? You know Mrs Allenby better than I do and you're the Kings' skipper. So you could be quite an influence on her.'

This time he tried to think carefully before he spoke at all. By now he was well aware of what this might mean to her. Moreover, he must do nothing to jeopardize their close friendship. 'Well, I think everything depends on how good you are. I mean, I've not seen you play in a team in a real match, have I? Lots of guys think they're OK until they come up against opponents who want to kick you to bits or are just, well, much better players. Then it's your character that matters as well as your talents, isn't it? Have you actually played for a team, Andi? A girls' team, maybe?'

She grimaced and shook her head. 'Not that

much, no. When we lived in Scotland I sort of played for a team but we weren't much good. Most of them were boys and too many of them just wanted to fool around when anybody looked like beating us. I definitely wouldn't want to play with just girls – that'd be a wee bit boring, I think. Boys' teams, like the Kings, are different: they definitely want to win all the time.'

'Want to is right – but we're not winning at the moment, are we?' murmured Kieren.

Andrea pounced. 'And that's what I'm talking about: the Kings and the way things are going just now. We're going downhill. We've got to have some new blood, we've got to start winning again. I could help with that; I know I could.'

'What about Oats – sorry, Frazer? What does he think about you playing for us?'

'Haven't asked him – well, not properly. I've hinted a bit but Frazer isn't good at picking up hints. Most boys are like that, actually. But we've trained so much together I think he'd say OK, go for it.'

Kieren nodded. 'Right, then, best thing would be if you came to a training session on

Tuesday night and joined in. If you like, I'll ask Jane to tell the other guys what's happening. Then if you put on a – a star performance you'll be in, won't you?'

'Great! Then – ' She was interrupted by a sharp rap on the bedroom door. They froze, just staring at each other.

'Hey, you two, got some news for you,' was Frazer's way of announcing himself. 'Can I come in?' Even before they could answer he waltzed in.

'So, what's this news you've got, eh?' Andrea asked in a tone that suggested he wasn't exactly welcome.

'Mum's just got back – didn't you hear her?'

'Er, no,' admitted Andrea.

'Well, here's the interesting bit,' Frazer went on. 'On the train she met this boy who's coming to live in Rodale Kings. And he's mad on football and Mum says that she thinks he might be quite good from the things he told her about the matches he's played in. So she's told him about the Goal Kings and when we train and where. So we'll probably meet him on Tuesday night. And everybody'll be really amazed.'

Frazer stopped at that point and waited for their reaction. He could tell that so far he hadn't entirely grabbed their attention; they were still more interested in each other than in anything else.

'Go on, then, brother, tell us the rest – I can see you're dying to,' Andrea invited. Frazer was wrong about one thing: she was very interested in his news because her first thought was that it might affect her hopes of playing for the Kings. If a talented newcomer turned up then Jane Allenby would be less likely to look for anyone else to add to her squad. It might be an excuse for her to reject the idea of playing a girl.

'He's Finnish – and I don't mean the end! He's from Finland,' Frazer disclosed eagerly. 'Mum says he looks a bit like Reuben because he's got such fair hair, except this boy's is more like the colour of straw.'

'Oh,' his sister and Kieren replied simultaneously. 'So, what's he doing here in England?' Andrea added.

'His dad works for one of the mobile phone companies, a big one. He's regional manager or something like that. The whole family's come over so Esko will be going to school here. Maybe our school. So that's it, folks.'

'Esko, that's a weird name,' commented Andrea, turning away to check her appearance in the mirror that was framed with images of frogs. 'What's his other name, Mr Know-It-All?'

'Actually, I don't know that, but you can ask him yourself if you can be bothered to come along to our training on Tuesday.'

'Oh, I can be bothered to do that all right,' Andrea replied spiritedly. 'I'll definitely be there.'

In his bedroom Sean Ferriby was also looking in the mirror. That was the only way he could examine the bruise on the back of his thigh, the injury inflicted by the Wasperton player who had been deservedly sent off for his savage tackle. It didn't hurt quite so much now, so perhaps the ointment he'd applied was having its effect. All the same, the wound was spectacular: mostly purplish-blue but some streaky orange and even a hint of green.

He heard the sound of a door opening downstairs. Hastily, he pulled his trousers on and prepared to go down to greet his mum and brother. Of course, she'd immediately want to know what he'd been doing and, just as inevitably, he would tell her that he'd been working on his plane. He had, too, but only for part of the time they'd been away visiting his sick grandmother (Sean had been on the previous visit so it had been his brother's turn tonight, thank goodness). Patrick thought that constructing models of aeroplanes, even if they did fly eventually, was a stupid way of spending time; but then Sean felt much the same about Patrick's devotion to snooker. If there was a game on TV nothing in the world would tear him away from it. 'I'm going to be *the* top player one day, you'll see,' he was forever boasting. 'I'll make a fortune. But you, you're just chucking money away all the time, building crazy old aircraft that crash and have to be repaired.' But then, Patrick knew nothing about the historic planes that had saved Britain in the Second World War, ones like the Lancaster he was patiently constructing at present. The brothers Ferriby agreed about hardly anything.

As he reached the bottom of the stairs he

caught his mother's penetrative gaze.

'Why're you limping?' she wanted to know.

'I'm not!' he exclaimed fiercely, the only way of defending himself. 'I'm walking perfectly normally.'

'Doesn't look like that to me,' she retorted. 'We've had enough injuries in this family without attracting any more. Are you sure you didn't do some damage in that game on Sunday? I know there was something bothering you that evening.'

'Mum, I'm fine. Maybe I got a bit of cramp or something. Tonight, I mean. Bending over to paint those tricky bits on the undercarriage.'

'You mean you *still* haven't finished that stupid bomber?' Patrick sneered.

Sean ignored him. One of these days, he vowed, he'd leave them all. He'd fly away in a plane that someone else had built and he'd never come back. Then never in his life would he have to share his room with a brother or anyone else.

'Well, if you've got any trouble at all I don't want you playing football again this Sunday,' Anna Ferriby returned relentlessly to the main subject. 'You ought to look after yourself, like

65

Patrick. He seems to manage his football well enough without always getting into trouble.'

Sean said nothing because it wasn't worth saying what he thought: that perhaps mothers' favourite sons could do no wrong because they always led a charmed life.

Kieren's parents were drinking coffee and casually watching the news on TV when Jakki returned to the subject of the Kings. Clark Kelly was quite used to his wife's deep interest in the football team and to some extent shared it. He'd even driven the hired coach when they'd all gone on a soccer trip to Scotland, but he didn't attend many matches, not least because his work in sales took him abroad for some lengthy spells.

'D'you know, I've been thinking about the team a lot and I've come to the conclusion they've lost confidence in Jane,' Jakki said. 'But for the life of me I can't think why that is. I mean, they're practically the same squad as last season. They haven't lost their skills – if anything, some of them seem better than last season. All right, Danny's lost his place, but Harry Greenland gets better almost by the match. He's a real find, that lad. I'm not sure about Dominic, mind you. Seems a bit aimless at times. Of course, I suppose it's a bit difficult for Jane to motivate *him*. She always says she treats him just like everybody else – oh, and they never talk about team matters at home. She says that's only fair.'

Clark gave a little shrug which might have indicated he didn't necessarily agree with that. When his wife was launched on one of her reviews of team affairs he usually didn't interrupt. In any case, he was inclined to agree with her.

'Then there's Davey and Reuben – they're definitely in good form. Of course, we all recognize that Davey is her all-time favourite. We've known that ever since she gave him the Player-of-the-Season Award, haven't we, even though we could all have made out a case for giving it to Kieren or possibly Danny.'

'Not sure about Josh,' she went on. 'I know he's scored some good goals but I still see him more as a defender. And that's where our previous coaches used to play him, isn't it? His height is a definite bonus when our defence is under siege.'

There was a pause while she considered what to say about other players. Clark took the opportunity to ask a question: 'Have you thought of telling Jane what you think? Especially about Josh – maybe even suggesting they swap places, he and Dominic. I know that Kieren once mentioned that Dominic had said he really fancied being a striker.'

Jakki shook her head vigorously. 'Don't think there'd be much point in that. She always listens very politely and says how pleased she is that we all care about the Kings. But she still sticks rigidly to her own ideas. Just like Ricky Todd did when he was coach. So, no point, as I say.'

'What's Kieren got to say? I mean, you must have discussed things with him. We're not like the Allenbys, are we, saying nothing at home about the Kings?'

'Well, I get the impression he agrees with me. He says Jane wants Frazer to keep to the left flank more, even though he's a natural right-footer. That could be causing gaps in defence. And he, too, thinks Dominic's lost some concentration. Mind you, I could make a good guess about what's worrying Dominic

– or attracting him, rather. Katie Stroud, Davey's sister. It's pretty obvious that he really fancies her and that she's, well, not exactly rejecting him! Yet I'm not sure that Jane has spotted it.'

'Trust you to spot the romance in life!' her husband smiled.

'Well, it's what makes the world go round, so they say. Didn't take Kieren long to fall for a girl, did it?'

Clark looked at his watch. 'I suppose he's with that girl now, isn't he? Well, I reckon it's getting a bit late for that sort of thing when he's got to go to school tomorrow. You know, Jak, I think he's spending more time with her these days than he does on his football. His game will suffer if this becomes a habit.'

'Oh, don't worry about that: soccer will always come first with him. You know how ambitious he is to play professionally and win caps in internationals, all that sort of thing. At his age, falling for a girl is just part of life – you must remember that!'

'Maybe,' her husband admitted, 'but I don't remember staying out as late as this on a date.'

'Oh, he'll be in in the next ten minutes, I'll

bet. He's not the one we have to worry about. It's the Goal Kings – and Jane.'

4 The Disappearing Player

Jane was worried about Sean but she didn't want to say or do anything that might embarrass him in front of his team-mates as they prepared to get changed for the away cup-tie with Redville Rangers. She thought he looked paler than usual, but that might simply be because he was starting this match rather than coming on as a sub. She suspected that his thigh wound was still troubling him a little, although he denied it. They'd had to miss the usual training session on the previous Tuesday because of the baby she'd had to deliver that evening. Now was not the time to ask to see the injury. Because it was so high on the leg probably none of the other boys had seen it either, so she couldn't ask any of them about it. All she could do was hope that Sean would get through the game without trouble.

Of course, she was just as worried about the

team as a whole: they weren't the Kings of old (well, of the previous season) and hard as she tried she still couldn't work out what was wrong with them. Perhaps, though, a good win over a top side would work wonders for them. Sometimes life could be as simple as that, for victory brought confidence and confidence could carry them to new heights.

'I know you want to win this match as much as I do,' she told them, standing in the middle of the wooden hut that acted as a changing-room beside the Redville pitch. 'After all, we've old scores to settle with Rangers, especially that 4–1 defeat earlier in the season. But that was the League and this is the Cup. This tie's come at a good time because we're not battling for vital League points. We've got a rest from that. So maybe you won't feel under so much pressure. I really hope so. I know it's an old cliché and you've heard it thousands of times because it's what all managers are supposed to tell their teams before almost every match, but I do hope you'll go out there and *enjoy* your football. If you enjoy it, you'll play well, I know you will.'

She paused and looked round the ring of

faces. None of them was smiling and only a couple, Kieren and Danny, managed a wan grin. Even Davey, normally as eager as anyone to get the game under way, was looking surprisingly serious. Dominic actually had his eyes closed but she couldn't comment on that without the risk of upsetting him. Then she focused on the newcomer to their ranks – and he returned her smile with interest. He might be her inspiration.

'By now I'm sure you've all had a chance to say hello to your new team-mate, Esko Hakkarainen – er, that is how you pronounce it, isn't it, Esko?'

'Oh yes, *very* good, Mrs Allenby,' he told her in a voice with an accent that sounded distinctly American.

'Good! I'm relieved to have got it right. Well, as I was saying, we're delighted that Esko has joined us. It was good of the Highlea League to allow us to sign him on special forms and I'm sure he'll be an asset. He's a sub today but I'm sure he'll be desperate to get on the pitch. So the rest of you'd better make sure you're not the one he replaces!'

As soon as she'd spoken she realized that

wasn't the most diplomatic thing to say to players already worried about the team's performances. But perhaps none of them had noticed. So she gave them her warmest smile, wished them good luck and left them to get changed.

The moment she appeared on the touchline Jakki Kelly rushed to her side. 'So, what're you going to do about Andrea, Jane?' she wanted to know.

Jane frowned. 'Andrea? Why, has something happened to her? Frazer didn't mention –'

'No, no. This idea of hers of wanting to play for the Kings. Hasn't she told you about it? Kieren seems to think you'll be all for it.'

'She certainly hasn't mentioned it to me. But, Jakki, I can't be thinking about that now. This is a vital match and I need to concentrate totally on that.'

'Jane, I understand that. It's just, well, I'd like to know if you're in favour of introducing a girl into the team. I mean, it'd have all sorts of effects on people, wouldn't it? Especially the boys themselves,' Jakki persisted.

'Of course it would, and that's why I can't give you a snap answer now. I'll have to think about it very seriously.' Jane paused, thought of something else and added: 'In any case, I've no idea whether Andrea can play at any level. I know she's keen on football, but that's all. Kieren should know better than any of us, I imagine. Those two spend a lot of time together, I gather.'

'Too much time!' Jakki replied sharply. 'Frankly, that's beginning to worry Clark and me.'

To Jane's relief the players emerged from the hut at that point and so she could break off from Jakki, whose worries could be put on hold. She was pleased to see that Esko was the centre of attention. Usually neither Davey nor Reuben had a lot to say for themselves but they appeared to be bombarding the Finnish boy with questions. Probably they wanted to know where he preferred to play. According to Sallie McKinnon, who'd been the first Kings supporter to meet him, Esko enjoyed being either a striker or a creative midfielder; and, of course, those were roles Davey and Reuben fulfilled for the Kings.

Sallie, mother of Frazer and Andrea, had told Jane on the phone as much as she'd gathered about Esko, and Jane herself had talked briefly with him. But, as nobody knew anything about the standards of junior football in Finland, it was impossible to forecast how good the boy with the straw-coloured hair and intelligent blue eyes might be. Jane was hoping that she might be able to play him at some stage of the match if only to see how he would react to his team-mates. Her fingers were crossed that he'd prove to be a real asset, for she'd learned from Serena Colmer that it was unlikely that Lloyd would return to the Kings. For the foreseeable future he was going to live with his dad away from Rodale Kings.

As the players warmed up with shooting and quick passing in the penalty areas Jane glanced warily along the touchline, checking whether Andrea was present but hoping not to catch her eye. But there was no sign of her, which was unusual these days.

In their red shirts with white sleeves and collars Redville Rangers were hitting the ball around with pace and assurance and there was an air of real confidence about them. That was understandable. In recent times they'd had some fierce battles with the Kings and usually emerged on top, even before their easy victory in the League this season. Greg Kingston, their coach, was a hard-talking, combative type and Jane had the impression he didn't much care for females in charge of boys' teams. So what would *he* make of a side that featured a girl in its ranks?

'Come on, you Reds, get stuck in!' he bellowed the moment Davey kicked off and slid the ball to Josh, who immediately trans-fered it to Reuben before dashing off towards the right flank. Moments later Davey was in possession again, only to be flattened prompt-ly by an opponent with a plainly damaged nose. Davey had expected that sort of treat-ment from Ollie because they'd had battles in the past; but he hadn't thought it would happen quite so soon. It all stemmed from the time Davey had been given a trial by Redville and Ollie, thinking Davey might replace him in Rangers' team in the future, did his best to sideline him. Ultimately, Davey remained with the Kings and that should have suited Ollie. But he still seemed to bear a grudge.

The ref issued a mild warning, Reuben took the free kick, floated the ball out to the right and Josh tore in to collect it. With clever footwork (which he hadn't demonstrated very often in the past) Josh wriggled past two opponents, flicked the ball against the shin of another, went past him and then, with superb judgement, slid a pass to the inrushing Sean. He'd thought he was giving the ball to Davey, but for once Sean's acceleration was the greater. Sean took the ball on for no more than a stride and then flashed a terrific and unstoppable shot into the top of the net.

'Oh, what a goal!' Jane sang out. Jakki, too, along with every other Kings' supporter, was applauding thunderously. This was the kind of start to a cup-tie they dreamed about but hardly ever saw in reality.

Sean was ecstatic. He hadn't often scored goals for anyone and none as good as this one. After breaking free of the celebrations of his team-mates he dashed over to the touchline and exchanged a few words with a woman wearing a black-and-brown coat, the collar turned up against the chill wind. Jane had never noticed her at any previous match but suspected she must be Sean's mum. Perhaps, later on, she'd be able to have a word with her.

It was always useful to have contact with players' families. Sean, she guessed, must have made a good recovery from his injury, for he was showing no sign of discomfort. But then, if you'd scored a goal like that, undoubtedly you would feel on top of the world.

Redville were rattled. They weren't used to conceding quick goals to anyone, let alone arch-rivals Rodale, against whom they had such an impressive record. With Greg Kingston roaring them on they swarmed forward in waves, trusting that sheer numbers would overwhelm the opposition. Ollie had sensibly recovered his composure and was spraying passes with great precision.

In the face of such an onslaught the Kings retreated. Worriedly, the defence began to pass the ball about among themselves, simply to retain possession. But that was lost when Kieren misjudged a sideways flick to Frazer and an opponent raced on to the ball. Looking up, the Redville attacker saw that his team-mate was homing in on goal, and the cross was perfect. The resultant header was only marginally less good but the outcome would still have been a goal if Icy hadn't produced a superlative save to tip the ball over the bar.

'Kieren, get a grip!' Jane yelled in exasperation. It wasn't the first mistake he'd made in the match and it was plain his concentration was poor. Normally, she hated to criticize players in public. Yet, sometimes, it was effective and because her skipper was rarely to be faulted it might work on this occasion. Deliberately, she didn't glance sideways to see what Jakki's reaction might be.

Thankfully, the corner was cleared with a powerful header from Dominic. He, at least, looked in good form. Still, it wasn't long before Redville were sweeping forward again. When they won a throw-in just in front of Jane it was taken by their red-haired midfielder, who appeared to have exceptionally long arms; he made good use of them by flinging the ball higher and further than any other schoolboy the coach had seen. Even Davey couldn't intercept the ball in spite of his leap and his positioning in front of an opponent several metres away (despite of his small build, the Kings' leading striker could rise like a salmon). The ball reached Ollie and he cleverly pulled it down with his left foot before turning and aiming for the top left-hand corner of the net. Nine times out of ten the ball would have sailed harmlessly over the bar when shot from that distance. This was the tenth time.

Icy had plenty of time to see the ball and his attempt to reach it almost succeeded. But the placing was perfect because the ball went into the roof of the net after brushing the angle of the crossbar and the far upright. Ollie disappeared in the avalanche of his team-mates. 'Just a fluke!' snorted Danny Loxham, who'd returned to stand close to Jane after his fruitless attempt to persuade Katie Stroud that she ought to go out with him that evening or any other time.

'No, it was unstoppable,' Jane admitted with her usual honesty, 'and I'm positive that's where the boy was aiming for. Harry did well to get as close to it as he did.'

That was the comment that convinced Danny he had no future whatsoever with Rodale Goal Kings. Nothing had gone right for him since the pre-season Presentation Evening when Jane had chosen to give the Player-of-the-Season Award to Davey, the award Danny believed should have been his.

Then he'd been injured and lost not only the captaincy but his girlfriend to Kieren. Now he sensed that his only hope of getting back into the team at all was an injury to Icy; and he wasn't going to wish that on anyone. He sauntered away from the group on the touchline.

Kieren was talking energetically to his co-defenders but there was no one he could blame for the goal. He'd heard his coach's stinging comment a few minutes earlier and he resented it; he knew he wasn't playing worse than anybody else so why should he be singled out for public abuse?

'Hey, you guys, we can get back into this game, no sweat,' Sean was saying, which surprised most of the Kings. Not only was he virtually a newcomer to the team, normally he didn't say much about anything at anytime. His goal seemed to have transformed him into a leader. 'Let's get at 'em right away.'

He set the example by hogging the ball when he got it, twisting one way, then another, not making much real progress but denying possession to Redville. Then, just after parting with it through a sharply angled pass to

Reuben, he became aware that his mum was calling to him from the touchline. She was putting away the mobile phone she'd been using and was signalling that he must come over to her. Desperately, he looked round to see if anyone else had noticed what his mum was up to; surely she couldn't expect him to drop out of the game to talk to her?

'Sean, this is an emergency!' she was yelling. 'We've got to go. NOW!'

'Mum, I'm playing in a game,' he gasped. 'What're you on about?'

'Patrick's been injured in his game,' she told him, reaching out to grab his arm and hold on to him so that he couldn't run back on to the pitch. 'It's bad news. We've got to go to him. And I need your help.'

He simply didn't know what to say or do. He glanced round again and was both thankful and alarmed to see that Mrs Allenby was hurrying towards them.

'What's wrong?' she wanted to know. 'You're interrupting the game – I'll have the referee on to me if Sean doesn't return to the pitch.'

'He's not going back, he's coming with me,'

Anna Ferriby announced. 'I'm his mum and I need him with me. His older brother's just been injured in the match he's playing in – heard about it on my mobile. He needs me and I need this one. We're going.'

'But – but we can't have a player leaving in the middle of a match,' Jane tried to point out. 'He's vital – you saw the goal he scored.'

Mrs Ferriby was already escaping, drawing Sean along by the arm until he managed to shake it off. 'My Patrick's health is more important than any football game,' she called over her shoulder. 'Anyway, football's just a load of grief these days.'

Jane could say no more. There was nothing she could do to stop Sean from departing. It was only later that she realized she could have suggested that someone else could take him home after the match, or take him wherever his brother and mother were. In the meantime, she had to talk to the referee. He'd blown his whistle to suspend play and was dashing towards her.

'What's going on here?' he inevitably wanted to know.

'A spot of bother at home; a crisis, really,'

replied Jane, her mind in turmoil. 'His mum's had to take him with her. So, er, well I'd like to put on a sub, if I may.'

The ref glanced at his watch. 'That's all right, but you'd better do it right away so we don't waste any more time. Tell me names and numbers.'

Jane looked down the touchline and summoned Larry Hill, a striker with more lows than highs in his appearances for the Kings. She didn't think he was much of a replacement for the newly inspired Sean Ferriby; all she could hope was that he'd use his height and determination to good effect in midfield. Certainly, he wouldn't be as pacey or inventive as the boy he was replacing.

'Good luck,' she said as she sent him on to the pitch. Luck, she reflected, was in short supply as far as the Kings were concerned. For this was the second successive match they'd lost a player in unusual circumstances – lost him in such a way that he'd departed from the ground even before the match finished. She knew she wasn't going to see anything more of Lloyd Colmer; so was the same going to happen to Sean Ferriby? He was a player who was just beginning to bloom and was surely going to be a real asset to the team for the rest of the season.

The Kings were jinxed. To Jane Allenby that seemed to be the only word that described the present situation. But how could you get over that? What could be done to change the team's fortunes? Jane admitted to herself that she simply had no idea what to do next, so perhaps this was the time to let someone else have a go. If she herself had lost control of the team then it was in everyone's interests that she should resign as the Goal Kings' coach.

When the ref blew for half time she steeled herself to try to deal with things as normally as possible. She couldn't quit in the middle of a match. That would be a body blow to her team and a gift to the opposition.

As the players drifted off the pitch and towards her she spotted that one of them was going in the opposite direction: Dominic. To her annoyance she saw that it was Katie he'd gone to talk to. 'Davey, will you please go and tell Dominic I want to talk to *everybody*. And that means him, too. He's over there with your sister,' she said crisply.

'Sorry, didn't know there was anything *urgent*,' Dominic muttered when he came over to join them.

'There's plenty to talk about that's urgent, especially in defence,' she told them. 'Half the time you're going to sleep, just like you did in the last match against Wasps. Concentration seems to have gone out of the window. You should all *know* how good Redville are and that we can't give them a millimetre to work in. You're giving them *acres*.'

'That's not true,' Kieren muttered. 'We're closing them down most of the time. Their goal was out of this world. They'll never score another like that.'

'Yeah, that's right,' Dominic put in. 'I *know* we're playing better than we did against Wasperton. You *must* have seen that!'

Jane was in a quandary. The last person she wanted to argue with in front of everyone else was Dominic. She was also remembering Jakki's earlier comment about her pessimism; maybe she *was* too inclined to look on the black side of things. The boys needed to be given a lift, not scolded like naughty children.

'I think we could improve,' she replied,

seeking a compromise. 'Look, I'm sorry I yelled at you, Kieren, but I have to repeat what I said about concentration. That *must* improve. We can win this match. Of course we can. We got one wonderful goal. Let's get another; let's turn on our best style.'

She knew that wasn't getting anywhere near the root of the problems affecting the team at present but optimism was needed. She also tried her brightest smile, but the glumness on the faces in front of her didn't disappear.

'What's happened to Sean?' Davey wanted to know.

Few expressions changed when she gave them a brief account of the Ferriby family's problems, although Reuben murmured: 'Well, we'll miss him. He was beginning to fit in with us really well.'

They did miss him, there was no doubt about it, as the second half got under way. Larry, eager to please as always, tried his best to slot into a left-sided midfield position but his first touch so often let him down; and when he did dispatch a pass to someone it was always the obvious option and so Rangers usually managed to intercept it. Jane had always told her team, especially defenders, to talk to each other, to alert other players to danger or the unsuspected close presence of an opponent. Now they were talking to one another, but mostly it was bickering: Kieren criticizing Frazer for not preventing a Redville pass from reaching an unmarked team-mate, Dominic snapping at Joe Parbold for missing an awkward header following a corner kick. Fortunately, that kick came to nothing, but any neutral observer at the match was bound to conclude that it was only a matter of time before the home side got the ball in the net again.

Jane glanced along the touchline, really looking for Danny who, she realized, hadn't been with the group for the half-time chat. There was no sign of him anywhere. But Esko caught her eye and grinned. Immediately she felt guilty again, for she had shamefully neglected him because of all her worries.

'Esko, what d'you think about our English football, then?' she asked, belatedly trying to make him feel welcome.

'OK, it's good,' he told her, his voice full of enthusiasm. 'I see good players here and good goals. Very fast, too.'

'Oh,' was all she could reply, a little surprised by his assessment. 'Is it not as good as this in Finland?'

He shrugged. 'Sometimes. But English football is what we all watch on the TV. We think your game is fantastic. That's why I want to play here, Mrs Allenby.'

That made her feel guilty again because she perhaps ought to have given him a chance in this game to show what he could do. And, at that moment, poor Larry got into trouble. Desperate to do something right after failing so many times to trap the ball or deliver a decent pass, he lunged heavily at an opponent on the ball, and that Redville player collapsed as if shot. Naturally, the ref saw it all and reached for his notebook. Jane thought the whole thing was due to Larry's clumsiness, that was all. He didn't deserve a yellow card. But he got one.

She looked at her watch; there was still time to put Esko on. Should she remove the hapless Larry? That would surely further undermine Larry's low self-esteem (which was partly due to the fact that it was his father who was forever promoting his son's cause). And, if

Esko's abilities didn't match his own claims, then the Goal Kings might be the losers. She decided to delay that decision for a little longer.

That delay proved to be fatal.

Another Redville raid was stemmed on the edge of the penalty area, but only at the expense of a free kick, when Dominic brought down their leading striker. In fact, the player actually tripped over when he lost control of the ball but the ref's interpretation was what mattered. He saw it as a foul. Rangers went through an elaborate kind of ritual when it appeared that two players wanted to take the kick but couldn't decide which one should. The Kings' defence clearly became unsettled by the time all this was taking – and then their wall broke up altogether when the Redville players collided. 'What idiots!' Kieren exclaimed and promptly moved out towards the ball.

That was the split-second that a third Redville player darted in and very cleverly lifted the ball into the box for a team-mate to streak through and nod it over Icy's shoulder into the top of the net.

'Hey, that's illegal!' Dominic protested as he and several Kings rushed over to the ref to get him to change his decision to award a goal.

'It was perfectly legal,' the official remarked calmly. 'They just outwitted you.'

Strictly speaking, he shouldn't have made a comment like that because it implied a form of favouritism. But nobody was so unwise as to point that out to him. By now, Redville supporters were celebrating as if they'd won the Cup itself. In most respects it hadn't been a great match, but the quality of the goals had lifted it.

'Oh no, not again,' Jane was murmuring to herself. It was clear that the Kings were going to lose again – and this time it meant they were out of the Cup. Although she'd not mentioned it to anyone, she'd been hoping that a good run in the Cup would act as a stimulus to the team and thus they'd start to do better in the League. Now, their season was in total disarray.

'That was a clever trick, I think,' Esko acknowledged. 'I wonder how many times they have done it. It looked very – what is the word? – oh yes, rehearsed, I think that is right.'

'It was rehearsed, I'm sure,' Jane agreed. 'Just wish I'd thought of something as effective as that. Oh, well, maybe I can adapt it for our own use later.'

She said that almost absent-mindedly because the future wasn't something she wanted to contemplate. At that moment all she could think about was that she'd failed the team again. She'd been outwitted by another coach. And she knew now that she should have given Esko his chance to show what he could do instead of favouring lumbering Larry.

Even as she decided she should make another substitution the final whistle sounded and the Goal Kings were out of the Cup. Redville and their supporters celebrated noisily as they'd become used to doing when playing against Rodale. As usual, Jane was on the touchline to greet her players as they came off and murmur consolatory words, but most of them avoided her eye. No one knew what to say about yet another defeat. Jane thought they looked crushed: that was really the only word for it.

She particularly wanted to have a few words

with Kieren, but he raced past both her and his mum, who was drifting towards Jane. With a wan grin Jakki remarked: 'These defeats are getting harder to take, aren't they? Honestly, I think we should have won this match. We had the chances, didn't we?'

Jane nodded and then said: 'Jakki, I'm sorry I yelled at Kieren. I mean, he wasn't really worse than anyone else in defence. I was just trying to wake everybody up.'

'Oh, don't apologize. You're the coach; it's your job to yell at people when you think they need it. I expect Kieren's feeling a bit low because he's missing Andrea. They're inseparable these days. But she's got this bee in her bonnet about being a player herself, so she's gone off today to see some other team that might be willing to take her on.'

Jane wasn't really listening. She'd made a decision and it was time to act on it.

'Jakki, are you going to be at home tonight? I mean, could you spare me a few minutes if I popped round to see you?'

'Well, yes, I don't think we've anything special on,' was the surprised reply. 'What've you got in mind?'

'I'd rather explain that later – now's not the time,' Jane replied cautiously. 'Oh, yes, will Kieren be there? Frankly, I'd rather just talk to you on your own without Kieren being involved.'

'Oh, you don't have to worry about him. He's bound to be in his room with Andrea or round at her place. Look, make it about seven if you can. We'll have finished eating by then and you and I can have a drink together.'

'Fine. See you then, Jakki. And thanks.'

5 Ringing the Changes

When Jane Allenby left the Kellys' house just before 8 o'clock that evening she wasn't sure whether she felt elated or down-hearted; probably it was a bit of both, she decided, as she walked towards her own home at a slow pace. Even though matters were now out of her hands she still had some serious thinking to do, some important decisions still to be made.

The first thing to do, she resolved, was to tell Dominic. She imagined that he might be quite pleased that his mum was no longer the coach of the team he played for; after all, as a family they could now talk about the Kings as much as they liked without anyone worrying about whether they were giving away secrets. She'd be able to ask him how he felt about his team-mates and whether they were enjoying making a fresh start under their new coach,

Jakki Kelly. Almost certainly Ken, Jane's husband, would feel happier about the change because he'd said more than once that she spent too much time worrying about the team and its troubles. She suspected that he felt those worries weren't helping Dominic to enjoy his football.

She also had to consider what to do about supporting the Kings in the future. Of course, she told herself, I'll always be cheering them on and thinking about them. In a way, they'll still be my team. On the other hand, she sensed it might be unfair to Jakki to turn up and simply stand on the touchline like any other regular supporter. If she did that, Jakki would be bound to feel that Jane was simply checking up on her or waiting to see if she made mistakes, especially mistakes of the kind that Jane herself wouldn't have made. No, it would be best if she stayed away, at least for the next few matches. She'd miss the atmosphere and the fun and the excitement of the games themselves, even though lately there hadn't been much fun in football for the Kings. A consolation was that at least Dominic would be able to give her an account of those matches.

Then, when Jakki felt secure in her new role, Jane would ask her if she minded her coming along to matches. That, all things considered, was the best course of action.

Jane was almost home when she got round to thinking more about Jakki herself. When she'd sprung the news on Kieren's mum she'd supposed that Jakki would accept immediately. In the time she'd known the Kelly family she'd always been aware how supportive of the Kings Jakki was, even though at times Jane suspected that Jakki's chief ambition was to help Kieren reach the top as a player. Yet, Jakki had clearly been astonished when Jane told her she was resigning as coach and was offering the job to her. Then she'd seemed strangely hesitant about accepting it. Was that because she didn't think she was capable of being coach? Or was she worried about the effect it might have on Kieren?

And what about Kieren: how would he react to having his mum as coach? For both of them it would be a tricky position, especially now that Kieren was the skipper, a role that Jane herself had given him.

Oh, well, Jane decided as she put the key in

her front door, that's no longer my problem.

'Jakki, for goodness' sake, sit down!' her husband pleaded. 'It's making me dizzy, watching you walk round and round the room like this. Just sit down, relax, put your feet up. You can make all your decisions just as comfortably that way.'

'But you know I think best on my feet, and I know I've got to be *at* my best to work out what to do *for* the best,' she replied neatly. All the same, she did as he asked and collapsed on her favourite recliner chair. 'You know, I still can't really take it in. I can't believe that Jane Allenby has packed up as coach just like that, without a hint beforehand of what she was going to do. D'you know, I wouldn't be one whit surprised if the phone rang in the next five minutes and she says "Sorry, I didn't mean it, I'll still be coaching the Kings in the next match against Denholm Avengers."'

Clark Kelly shook his head. 'Jak, she'll do nothing of the sort. You know what a fair-minded person she is – everybody thinks that. So she'll not go back on her word. Things have gone badly for the team and she's honest enough to recognize that she herself must be partly responsible. As she's just said to us, what the team needs is a new leader with new ideas. And she chose you. She knows how much the Goal Kings mean to you – well, to both of us.'

'Well, OK, I accept I've got the job now of lifting the boys. It's just that I've got to find a way to do it. It's not going to be easy.'

'Jak, it's not like you to lack confidence. Nobody who was once the lead singer in a rock group can possibly lack confidence!'

'That was a long time ago,' she acknowledged with a faint smile, 'and this is a very different game, literally. Remember, too, I'm following somebody who won the Championship with these players, or most of them, anyway. So whatever I do she's a hard act to follow.'

'Don't forget you've got something in common that ought to be to your advantage,' Clark pointed out. 'Your own son's in the team, and in your case he's the captain. So at least you'll be able to talk things through with him and see what his ideas are and so on.'

Jakki's hand had flown to her mouth and

her eyes opened wide. 'I can't believe it! I haven't thought about him until this moment. I was so amazed by Jane's resignation that everything else flew out of my head. What on earth is he going to say when I tell him?'

Her husband didn't answer immediately. Then, softly, he gave his view. 'Not sure how he'll react. He's getting harder to read these days, particularly since that girl came on the scene and snaffled him up. But I think he needs to know pretty quickly from you before he finds out from anyone else. It'll be easier on him that way.'

The Kings' new coach took a quick look at her watch. 'I'd better ring him, then. I mean, he won't be home for a while yet, judging by recent evenings. I just hope someone answers when I ring the McKinnons.'

But no one did answer because the line was engaged. That was annoying. Jakki resented not being able to get straight through to the person she wanted. A couple of minutes later she tried again. Same result. Five minutes after that she was still out of luck. Clearly, someone in the McKinnon household was having a long chat. Frustrated, Jakki decided she must ring somebody. So she dialled a different number.

Davey Stroud put down the phone. He was feeling a little dazed by what he'd just heard but was still aware that his sister, sitting on the opposite side of their lounge, was looking at him with eager curiosity. She'd been pretending that she was watching a TV comedy programme, a favourite of hers, but she hadn't laughed once.

'Was that Dominic's mum you were talking to?' she asked him. She could have said 'Mrs Allenby' or 'the Kings' coach' but it was sheer pleasure to be able to say her boyfriend's name aloud.

He nodded.

'And?' she demanded.

'And what? Katie, she was talking to me, about football, about the Kings.' He paused, still trying to come to terms with what she'd said.

'So that affects me, too. You know Dominic and I are, well, best mates. You've made enough jokes about it. Look, I know you like to keep things to yourself, Davey, but this is different.' She knew she was on the verge of pleading, but that couldn't be helped. In any case, when he knew you really needed his help, he gave it. As brothers go, Katie had recently concluded, he wasn't all that bad.

He moved over to the red-and-blue sofa, sank down at one end and then swung his feet up to lie full length, with his head on cushions. His sister forbore to point out, as their mother would have done, that he hadn't first removed his outdoor shoes. His startlingly blue eyes were focused on a painting of a beach scene on the far wall. Mostly when he looked at it he liked to imagine that it was somewhere in Italy, not far from the Serle 'A' club he would play for and score so many goals that he'd become a legend in European football. Now, however, he wasn't even seeing the painting.

'Well, if you must know,' he said in a low voice, 'Mrs Allenby's given up as coach. She says she doesn't think she can do any more to lift us up the League. She says she's failed us, so she's packed up the job.'

Katie's hand had flown to her mouth. 'But, but what about Dominic? I mean, he's vital to the team, isn't he? He might not want to play for the Kings if his mum goes somewhere else.'

'Oh, I don't think that's going to be a problem for him,' Davey replied with a wry smile. 'He might be a lot happier if his mum isn't there. I know he's always been a bit worried that the rest of us might think he's carrying tales from the dressing-room back to his mum. You know, that he's a sort of spy.'

'Dominic would never be a spy,' Katie stated with total conviction. 'He's not like that in anything.'

'Oh, I'm sure you'd know,' her brother agreed. 'Anyway, that will be somebody else's problem now. Kieren's, actually.'

She was thoroughly puzzled by that. 'Kieren? What's this to do with him?'

'Just that it's his mum who's going to be our new coach. That might make things a bit tricky for him in future.'

'Jakki Kelly's taking over? Wow, that'll be interesting – for everybody, I mean. D'you think Kieren will give up the captaincy? That's the job you wanted when Danny lost it, isn't it?'

He nodded. 'I still do want it. And –'

'Hey, I think I'd better ring Dominic, see how he's feeling. I know he's at home to-night. So –'

'Hang on, I've got somebody I need to ring first,' Davey cut in. And his customary speed off the mark on the pitch was just as effective in the family lounge. He reached the phone before Katie was even half-way across the room.

'Have you been talking to everybody else in the team?' Davey asked when at last he could get through to the McKinnon household. 'Honestly, it's been like a marathon, trying and trying and trying.'

'Oh, sorry, but it's Mum,' Frazer explained. 'When she gets launched on a chat with Kirsty – that's a friend of hers back in Scotland – they never stop until they run out of breath or something. The rest of us might just as well go to bed! Anyway, what is it you want to talk to me about, Davey?'

'If you haven't been on the phone yourself, does that mean you haven't heard the big news, then?' Davey wasn't able to keep the excitement out of his voice when he realized that he could be the one to break it to his team-mate.

'What big news?' enquired Frazer, supplying the question his caller wanted to hear.

'Mrs Allenby's resigned as coach and Mrs Kelly is taking over! News from the Kings doesn't come much bigger than that, does it? Jane told me this herself.'

'Aye, you're spot on there, Davey. That's pretty amazing, all right.' None the less, Frazer sounded quite calm.

'You're *sure* you haven't heard this from anyone else, Oats? I mean, did Kieren phone earlier and drop a hint, or something like that?'

'No way. Kieren's here, as usual. Been with Andi all evening – as usual. If he'd known, he wouldn't have kept it to himself.'

'So you could go and tell him, then, Oats. Then you could let me know what he says. I mean, he might not want to be skipper any more now his mum's the coach. And she might not want him to be. That could be one of the changes she'll be making.'

'Could be, but somehow I doubt it, Davey. Anyway, I'll go up and let them know, see what they say. So thanks for letting me know. Cheers.'

After putting down the phone he paused for a few moments, thinking about what he'd just learned. He didn't imagine that his own role in the team was at risk. In spite of the Kings' poor results he and Kieren had forged a good partnership. Well, they had in Mrs Allenby's eyes, because she'd said so. Still, it would be important to keep up his good relationship with KK on all fronts.

Tentatively, he tapped on Andi's bedroom door. 'Sorry to break in on you guys again,' he said just loudly enough for them to hear, but hopefully not so loud that his mum would overhear it. 'But this is really important. You need to know about it.'

There was a predictable pause before Kieren replied. 'Hang on a sec, Oats.' Then Andi opened the door.

'Fray, this is becoming a rather annoying habit,' she said quietly. 'So what is it this time? It'd better be something *good*, or . . .'

'Kieren will have to judge that,' he said, following his sister into the room. 'This is it: your mum's taken over as coach of the Kings because Mrs Allenby has packed up the job.'

It was gratifying to see the astonishment on KK's face. He'd been lying back on the bed, but those words galvanized him into sitting up immediately and then swinging his legs to the floor. There was no doubt whatsoever in Frazer's mind that his team-mate had known nothing of this development. Andi, too, was wide-eyed and temporarily speechless.

'Is this a wind-up, Oats?' Kieren asked, eyes narrowing. 'Where'd you hear this?'

'Davey Stroud just phoned and he'd been told by your mum in person. So it's not a joke.'

'But why didn't your mum tell you first, K?' asked Andrea, recovering the power of speech. 'I mean, that's a bit rotten, letting you hear it from someone else.'

Before Kieren could try to work that out, Frazer supplied a possible reason. 'Mum's been on the phone for half a century tonight, so if anyone tried to phone us they'd be out of luck. And maybe your mum did try. Davey said all this had happened tonight, anyway.'

Kieren had started to prowl round the small room like a caged tiger. 'I don't get it,' he muttered. 'Why's Jane given up? I mean, I know results have been bad but, well, we'll start winning again soon. Bound to.'

'But your mum. Well, she'll be sure to want to change things a wee bit, or maybe a lot,' Andrea pointed out. 'All new coaches do. That's why teams get new coaches, to switch things about. I mean, maybe she'll like the idea of having a girl in the side. Don't you think so, KK?'

'Doubt it,' he replied fairly abruptly. 'Mum's never shown any interest in girls' soccer. She never played for anybody when she was a kid – she once told me that. Listen, I'll have to get hold of her, see what's going on.'

'Are you going home now, K?' Andi asked eagerly. 'I mean, I should come with you and then I can talk to her about – well, about the team.'

Kieren glanced at his watch and immediately looked surprised. 'Don't think you'd better. It's a bit late. Anyway, it'd be better if I talked to her first. I am the skipper, aren't I?'

'So you've got plenty of influence with her. That's important. Tell her – tell her what we've decided, you and me. Promise, Kieren.'

He turned back to kiss and hug her and Frazer tactfully looked away, although remaining in the room. Kieren then gave him a quick glance before agreeing to do as his girlfriend asked. 'Of course I'll tell her, Andi. And I'll make sure she listens. Cheers, then. See ya, Oats.'

It was the following day before Sean heard the news about the changes. That was when Davey stopped him in the corridor at Rodale High and asked him how he felt about it. Sean really didn't know what to say because he couldn't admit he was worried that a new coach might not want him in the team.

So he took the easy way out and said: 'Not sure. What about you, Davey?'

'She's bound to make changes, isn't she? All new football managers do. That's why they get the job.'

'But you'll be all right, Davey. You're our top goal-scorer, aren't you, so nobody would drop you. You're so *confident*,' Sean told him, not holding back his obvious admiration.

'Oh, you can't say that,' Davey responded, although his manner belied his words. 'Not one player in our team at present is guaranteed his place. We're not winning, I'm not scoring enough goals, even Kieren's form has dipped. So somebody's bound to be dropped.'

'Yeah, bound to be,' Sean agreed gloomily. He was thinking how unfair it would be if he was a victim. After all, he'd more or less recovered from his thigh injury (the discoloration was hardly noticeable now) and he was sure he was in good form on the pitch. His brother Patrick hadn't been hurt as seriously as his mother feared and she'd even apologized to Sean for taking him so hastily from the Kings' game against Redville.

But then, 'life's unfair' was a phrase he heard constantly from the lips of various adults as well as from his mum's. The unfairest cut of all would be if he lost his place to a complete newcomer, the Finnish boy Esko, who, Sean would have to concede, had looked really good in a lunchtime kickaround alongside the school pitch.

Danny had been hoping that it would be Jakki who answered when he rang the Kelly household that evening. He'd worked out very carefully how to congratulate her on her new role and assure her of his support in future. He'd decided that he might as well mention that, as of course she knew, he used to be captain and he'd be perfectly happy to take over again if she needed him. If he put the idea in her mind that he *could* be skipper again, then she might consider it. He wasn't going to risk a situation arising where it never occurred to her that a change of captaincy could help the team to prosper again.

While he was waiting for someone to pick up the phone he reflected for the umpteenth time that his life these days always seemed to depend on what females decided. He'd lost two girlfriends, Sophie and then Andrea, because they'd chosen to go out with someone else. Then Jane Allenby had taken the captaincy away from him. And now his future in the Kings' team was in the hands of Mrs Kelly. One of these days, with a bit of luck, there'd be a man in charge of his football again.

Of course, it turned out to be Kieren who answered the phone. 'Oh, hi, Danny, how's things?' he greeted him cheerfully enough. But then, Kieren could afford to be cheerful because he'd got the girl that Danny wanted.

'OK. Listen, I was just wondering whether your mum was planning any big changes for our next match.' As soon as he heard Kieren's voice he decided he might as well be just as direct in his approach with him.

'Er, I don't really know, Dan. We haven't discussed it. I expect she'll do something, but she's out tonight with some of her mates. They're all singers and they're supposed to be doing a performance for charity at Christmas.'

Kieren had by now worked out what Danny wanted and he kept talking in order to think what to say next. But he hadn't predicted the question that the Kings' reserve goalkeeper did ask.

'D'you think you'll still be skipper now your mum's in charge? D'you think you *should* be? Having the captain and the coach in the same family seems a bit much to me.'

For a few moments Kieren simply didn't know how to answer that, not least because he still experienced twinges of guilt that he, and not Danny, was both Andrea's boyfriend and captain of the Kings, roles that previously Danny had cherished. Yet Andrea had come to him of her own volition and it was Mrs Allenby who'd decided that he should be skipper.

'Danny, mate, you'll have to ask my mum that,' he said eventually, his team-mate having patiently awaited a reply without prodding for one. 'I quite like being captain but I won't go mad if I have to give it up. And if I do lose it, well, I'd rather you had it than anyone else. Honest.'

'And I'd like it back, so we'll see what happens. See ya, Kieren.'

But he wasn't to see the present Kings' captain quite as soon as he assumed he would.

6 Going It Alone

Jakki Kelly was so astounded by the message she'd just heard on her answerphone that she had to play it again a couple of times to take it in. 'Mum, it's me,' came the unmistakable voice of her only son. 'I know I'm messing you about and I'm sorry, honestly. I'm letting you down. But I've just got to go with Andrea to her match today, got to. She's got to come first today. The Kings can still win without me. I'm sure they will win with you in charge. So best of luck, Mum. See you this afternoon, OK?' There was a momentary pause and then the final words: 'Oh, and Danny would be a great choice to take my place as skipper, Mum. Cheers, then.'

How could he do this to her, abandon her, and the team, only an hour or so before her first match as coach of Rodale Goal Kings? He *knew* how much this game against Denholm

Avengers meant to her and to his team-mates. He *knew* the Kings needed to put out their strongest side because victory was vital in their present plight so near to the foot of the League table. He *knew* she needed all the support she could get in doing a job she'd never done before, one in which the support of family and friends was essential.

Yet he'd walked out on her: literally walked out on her. Casually, at breakfast, he'd announced that he had to nip round to Andrea's to collect something; of course, she'd told him not to be back late and he'd just nodded. Now, it seemed to her, he'd timed things perfectly, knowing very well that she normally had a bath before she went out to anything important. Because his father had already gone out to play golf, Kieren had known when the answerphone would be on. Clark had said that he planned to get back in time to attend the Kings' game, but Kieren was the one she needed there, not least because he was her top defender as well as captain. Oh Kieren, she lamented inwardly, to let me down today of all days. How *could* you?

Then she shook her head to clear it of

unhappy thoughts and focused on what had to be done to make up for her son's absence. Too many changes would unsettle any team, especially when they had a new coach to work with, and so she'd intended keeping them to a minimum. She'd already discussed her ideas with the players concerned and was delighted they'd welcomed them. Well, most of them approved. Josh Rowley, however, hadn't been at all keen on returning to play in defence. As he pointed out to her, he'd always been good up front and Mrs Allenby had only recently restored him to the attack. 'But we need your height and experience in the back line, Josh, we really do,' Jakki had pointed out as winningly as possible. 'I promise you this, if it doesn't work out, you won't be dropped. You can revert to being a striker. Remember, everything I'm trying is for the good of the team. And you've always been a team man, I know that.' Josh had nodded and promised he'd do his best.

Dominic, on the other hand, was delighted to know that he was to be tried as a striker again, a role he'd enjoyed in the past with other teams. He wasn't as tall as Josh, but he was very strongly built and Jakki felt he could hustle effectively in the penalty area alongside Davey and Reuben.

Equally thrilled by his role was Sean Ferriby, a player who'd impressed Jakki (and had also won her sympathy when his mum hijacked him from the last match). She wanted him to play further forward, supporting the main strikers and creating openings for himself whenever chances arose. Now that Kieren was missing she'd have to draft someone else into defence and Gareth Kingstree was the obvious candidate because he'd played there previously. Fleetingly, she thought about trying the new boy, Esko, in the back line. However, she really knew nothing about his talents and this wasn't the time to take risks.

As she drove to the football ground she remembered the last thing Kieren had said about the captaincy. Well, she supposed she'd have to appoint somebody. Danny, though, wasn't a possibility because he wasn't going to be playing today. She hadn't talked to him as much as Jane had, so she wasn't as aware of his qualities as an enthusiast and leader and diplomat. In any case, Jakki was quite happy with Icy Greenland in goal, so there was no need to replace him. Finally, she wasn't going to indulge her absconding son by letting *him* have his choice as the new captain.

So, who should she give the armband to? Dominic might have been suitable but now he was playing up front he had enough to think about. Actually, now she considered it, the captaincy was probably best held by a defender rather than a striker; a defender saw more of what was happening on the pitch in front of him whereas a striker necessarily had a more limited view. Now she was down to two candidates: Joe Parbold and Frazer McKinnon. Joe, though, was not much of a talker in any circumstances; he was solid, dependable, but probably uninspiring. So it had to be the chirpy Scot, Frazer. Jakki tried to put it out of her mind that he was Andrea's brother because he shouldn't be overlooked for that reason alone. There was something, however, that she would ask him when she gave him the armband.

Most of the players had arrived ahead of her and she greeted them all with her brightest smile. Confidence, she believed, was transferable: if you looked good and gave the impression you knew what you were doing then others would follow your example. Fortunately, most of the boys thought she was by far the prettiest of all the mothers they knew and so they responded with similar warmth. They were also, though they admitted this only among themselves, impressed by the fact that she had been a celebrity once as the lead singer in a rock group.

'Just before I come and have a last word with you in the changing-room, I need a word in private with Frazer,' she announced. So far, nobody had asked her a single question about anything. One or two raised their eyebrows or looked mystified, but they trooped off without comment.

'Frazer, did you know in advance that your sister and Kieren were going off together this morning?' she asked crisply.

He sounded as startled as he looked. 'Going *off* together? Where? I mean, what *for*?'

'That's what I was hoping you'd tell me. He left a message on the answerphone saying he was going to a match with Andrea and that's why he wouldn't be playing for us. I find this as hard to believe as obviously you do.'

'Oh, that,' Oats murmured as if it was something not worth talking about. 'It's just a girls' match, a sort of trial for Andi. She's hoping she'll be able to play regularly. Kieren's there to support her, I suppose. I expect he'll be back for our next match, Mrs Kelly.'

There was a steely look in Jakki's eyes. 'Well, that will depend on whether I'm prepared to have him in the team after this . . . this betrayal. I'll have to think about that. Frazer, we now need a new captain and I think you'd be good at the job. So, how about it?'

'Me?' That invitation surprised him even more than the news of Kieren's defection. At the same time he felt a tingle of excitement. 'Well, I'd like that fine, I really would. D'you mean for good?'

'Again, I'll have to think about that in the light of what happens today and – and when Kieren gets back. We'll take things a match at a time – isn't that what coaches are always supposed to say?'

Frazer grinned. 'Aye, I can tell you're getting into the swing of things, Coach!'

When she and Frazer reached the dressing-room she gave the rest of the team the news and watched their reactions. Most of them simply looked surprised, but recovered quickly to congratulate their Scottish team-mate. Judging by his expression. Davey was the most disappointed and Jakki supposed he'd probably have been given the job if Jane had still been in charge and Kieren had let her down. Until he moved towards the door she hadn't realized that Danny was even in the room. She was going to say something to him about being a sub today but he moved too quickly for her. 'Danny!' she called to him. But he simply muttered that he'd 'forgotten something' and disappeared.

She hoped that didn't mean that she'd now lost the services of her reserve goalkeeper, but she wasn't going to chase after him.

The rest of the team were still looking at her as if expecting further announcements. For her part, she glanced at her watch and said: 'Shouldn't you be getting changed, all of you? The ref will be calling you out for the kick-off in a couple of minutes.'

No one answered and suddenly she sensed

what was wrong. They were waiting for her to leave. 'Oh, right. Well, I'll be getting off,' she told them. 'Remember what I told you when we completed the training on Tuesday night: this is the most vital match in the Goal Kings' history. So make sure you're in top form. We've beaten Denholm Avengers before and we're going to beat 'em again. *Today*. Best of luck, boys.'

She couldn't help wondering how different a message that was from what Jane would have delivered in the same circumstances. She'd intended to ask Kieren about such matters on the way to the ground but, of course, he'd chosen to be absent. Of course, she could have asked Jane herself, but they hadn't been in touch since Jane's dramatic visit a week ago to Jakki's house. There hadn't even been a 'good luck' message from her predecessor; but then, perhaps Jane intended to convey that in person this morning.

However, when she surveyed the scatterings of spectators there was no sign of Dominic's mum. Perhaps, though, Jane was simply being tactful, which was typical of her. No doubt she'd turn up at future matches, for her loyalty to the team wouldn't change. Jakki couldn't see Clark, either, and that caused her a pang of annoyance. Here she was, in charge of her first game as a soccer coach, and neither her son nor her husband was present to support her. Still, one or two of the Kings' regular fans made a point of coming up to congratulate her and wish her luck.

In spite of what must have been embarrassment over her daughter's disappearance with Kieren, Sallie McKinnon came to speak to her. 'It's really good of you, Jakki, to make Frazer the skipper,' she said warmly. 'I know he's absolutely thrilled by it.'

'That's good,' Jakki responded. 'He's been playing well and this may help him to do even better.' She realized that nothing was being said about either Kieren or Andrea, so probably it was best to leave it that way.

One thing that had surprised her was the presence of so many spectators sporting red-and-white scarves and other favours. When Denholm Avengers emerged from the dressing-room she saw why: they had switched from their pale blue strip of previous seasons to red-and-white stripes on their shirts and black shorts. Somehow that made them look a good deal more aggressive. Would it also provide them with a change of luck against the Goal Kings?

'Oh, no!' she upbraided herself. 'If you go on thinking like this you'll finish up riddled with superstitions, just like Jane Allenby. Stop it!'

In fact, luck was distinctly not on the side of the Kings in the opening exchanges. Just as his coach hoped he would, Sean fought for possession and then set about creating openings for Davey and Dominic as well as for himself. Like Davey, he had excellent balance, energy and pace; his additional asset was that he could tackle like a lion hunting a meal. Emerging from the first mêlée with the ball he took it forward before finding Davey with the perfect pass to run on to: exactly the sort of ball that Davey craved and sometimes received from Reuben.

Davey ran, swerved, swung in a half-circle, dragged the ball cleverly behind one foot before switching it to the other, and then raced past a stupefied opponent. Dominic was slow to catch up or catch on to what was being intended, so it was Davey himself who then cut into the box to meet the advancing goalkeeper, Gary Fixby, one of the best in the Highlea Sunday League. It was a situation Davey had created umpteen times and he drew his opponent towards him before suddenly swerving sharply to his left to take the ball round him. Gary had already committed himself to his dive to smother the ball, or even to take it off Davey's toes. He missed it, his hand caught Davey's ankle and the Kings' top striker went tumbling across the penalty area.

'Penalty! Must be,' Jakki yelled. And hers wasn't the only voice making that claim. Avengers fans were silent. In their hearts, most of them knew what the decision would be.

Yet, the referee simply shook his head in response to appeals from the Kings. He'd appeared to hesitate before deciding anything and then gave a goal-kick. Davey and Sean were livid and Jakki half-feared they'd be cautioned for protesting too much, but they escaped with a finger-wagging. Perhaps, Jakki decided, all this had happened just too early in the match. If it hadn't been the first minute the ref might have awarded a penalty or shown yellow cards.

The Avengers certainly took heart from that let-off and soon were bombarding Harry Greenland with shots from all distances. Thankfully, none beat him. On the other hand, the Kings' strike force soon began to give the impression they'd lost touch with each other following that first-minute disappointment. Dominic, in particular, looked sluggish and his challenge for the ball lacked the sort of authority he'd normally displayed in defence. Even Davey's pace was slower and it occurred to Jakki that he might have suffered some injury from that tumble in the box. Sean was working hard and twice had shots on target, only to see them confidently scooped up by Gary, whose father, Jonathan Fixby, was Denholm's coach. He was already on record as saying that he thought Gary would play for England one day.

The game was still scoreless at half-time. In customary fashion, the players gathered round their coach to hear any comments or fresh instructions. Jakki realized she had no new ideas about how her team might end their goal drought, so all she could do was offer encouragement for an improved second half. She knew she could tinker with the make-up of the side but it was hardly fair to make Dominic and Josh switch places after so short a time in their new roles.

'Anyone got any good ideas for the second half?' she asked, trying to sound both serious and light-hearted.

She sensed that was a mistake when no one replied at all until Josh muttered: 'Score some goals and win the game.' No smiles greeted that remark and, indeed, both Davey and Reuben glared fiercely at their former fellow-striker, although they didn't actually say anything to him.

'Well, good luck, anyway, boys,' Jakki said as the ref signalled to the teams to return to the pitch.

The stagnation, however, continued. Recent rain had turned the centre of the pitch into something of a glue-pot and that was where most of the play took place. 'Use the wing!' Jakki yelled at Sean when he managed a breakaway. Unhappily, he either didn't hear or he ignored her as he turned infield again and predictably lost the ball to a slithering tackle. When he got up he explored the back of his thigh but kept moving. A few minutes later, Dominic reacted angrily after being brought down and this time the referee's hand went to his pocket to bring out a yellow card. Jakki wondered whether now was the time to replace him. Larry Hill, however, was her only striker among the subs and she thought little of his abilities. Dominic remained where he was.

During a lull in play she took a longer look along the touchline, but there was no sign of her husband, Clark, or of Jane Allenby. By this stage of a game she herself would have been alongside the coach, exchanging views and comments, and she wished that Jane were here now so that they could chat. Even other parents and spectators seemed to be keeping their distance and Jakki felt thoroughly isolated.

Only a couple of minutes remained when Joe Parbold was injured in a clash in the Kings' penalty area. Both he and his opponent went down heavily and then half sat-up, each holding his head in his hands. After the quickest of glances the ref signalled to the touchline for the coaches to come on.

That was the moment Jakki realized she hadn't made any provision at all for medical attention in case of incidents like this. She had remembered to put a sponge in her bag, but that was all. Dry-mouthed, and praying that this wasn't a serious injury, she dashed on to attend to Joe, perhaps the most reliable of all the Kings' defenders and known fittingly to his team-mates as The Rock. He was shaking his head and looking a trifle dazed as Jakki asked him how he was feeling. 'Er, a bit sort of woozy,' he murmured.

She helped him to his feet and then used the sponge to clear away some mud from his forehead and temple. What else she could do she had no idea. All she could think about was getting him off the pitch and finding someone else to provide treatment.

'Your physio not here today? Jane, isn't it?' someone was asking her. It was Jonathan Fixby, her opposite number.

'Er no, afraid not,' Jakki replied. She couldn't admit that she herself was supposed to be in charge.

'Well, I'll have a look at your boy, if you like; check there's no concussion,' the Avengers' coach offered.

'That's very kind of you, *very* kind,' Jakki told him with feeling.

Thankfully, he could find nothing wrong with Joe or his own player and so both were given the all-clear to continue by the ref without having to leave the pitch. Jakki thought that her central defender was still looking a bit unsure of himself when next he had the ball and so she made her first substitution.

'Esko, I want you to fill in for Joe in the back line,' she told the Finn. 'Don't go rushing forward or anything like that. Keep back, just make sure the opposition don't get past you.'

'But I play as a forward or in midfield,' he pointed out. 'I do not defend.'

'I *need* you in defence, so that's where you're going,' she snapped. 'Are you playing or not?'

He blinked at her tone. He knew there was only a minute or so left. Maybe it was best not to argue with a new coach. 'Oh, sure,' he smiled. 'OK.'

Like the match itself, his smile didn't last much longer. For in the time that remained

Esko didn't get so much as a single touch of the ball. When the ref blew for time neither side had scored and nobody took much satisfaction from the game.

'Well, I suppose one point is better than nothing,' Jakki remarked consolingly to her disappointed team. They nodded, but no one had much to say; even Esko kept his sense of grievance to himself for the present. 'We'll talk about things on Tuesday evening,' she promised.

After shaking hands with Jonathan Fixby and thanking him again for his help during the match she drove home, reflecting on the fact that at least she'd not lost her first game as the Kings' coach. Her thoughts were also on Kieren and how she was going to deal with him.

He'd reached home ahead of her and for once Andrea wasn't with him. She thought he would be in a defiant mood because he knew he was in trouble with her, but he wasn't. He repeated his telephone apology and then asked about the match, who'd played, what had happened and even how she'd felt about being coach. So she gave him the details and her views and then, taking a deep breath, switched to the matter of his desertion.

'Any player, whoever he is, has to be punished for walking out on his team-mates,' she pointed out. 'In a way, it's even worse with you because you're the captain. When we're in a crisis like this one the last thing I want is to lose my best player. But I've no option, Kieren. So I'm suspending you for two matches. And, of course, everybody will be told why you're out of the team.'

She saw him swallow but, to her surprise, he didn't protest. 'OK,' was all he said.

'Oh, and you've got to attend the matches you miss,' she added. 'There's to be no sneaking off to other games with Andrea. Understood?'

He nodded. 'Wouldn't happen, anyway. Andi got injured today, really nasty kick on her knee. A supporter had to give her a lift home. We both reckon she won't be playing again for, oh, at least a couple of weeks.'

'Oh, I'm sorry to hear that,' his mum sympathized. 'But I'd better tell you now, I don't see a place for her in our team. Yes, I know how keen she is to play in a good team, but I

can't risk the consequences, *possible* consequences, I admit, of having a girl playing for
us, however talented she may be. We've got
enough problems at present, Kieren.'

Once again, he accepted her decision without argument. That just wasn't like him. 'Are
you all right, darling? I mean, apart from what
we've just been talking about?'

'Yeah. Just worried about Andi, that's all. I'll
be going round to see her later. She may need
to see the doc tomorrow. That's what they
think.'

Jakki didn't see any point in trying to forbid
such a visit; that would be sure to store up more
trouble for them all. 'Well, give her my love and
tell her I hope she'll soon be better.'

'Thanks, Mum, I will.' And she felt he was
really grateful.

Her next concern was Clark: why hadn't he
kept his promise to attend the match? His
answer when he returned home an hour or so
later surprised her. 'No, I wasn't held up or
anything like that, Jakki. I simply stayed away
so that you could do things in your own way.
You had to make your own decisions without
reference to me. I'm sure that was for the best,

whatever happened. So tell me, how did it go?'

Later, when she had time to herself again, she concluded that her husband had been right. On the other hand, she wasn't at all sure that the changes she'd made to the team were the right ones. After all, the Kings hadn't won. Still, maybe things would improve with the next game against Friday Bridge, a side they had a particularly good record against.

They didn't, they didn't improve at all. Once again, the Kings failed to score. In part, Jakki put that down to a fit of sulks from Davey Stroud. It started with something as insignificant as a throw-in to the opposition. She noticed that when Davey marked an opponent who might receive the ball, he was usually unable to reach it because he simply wasn't tall enough. Before that could happen again, Jakki yelled to him to move aside so that Dominic could mark the likely recipient. It worked, and Dominic managed to make the interception. Then, a few minutes later, when there was a break in play, Davey darted to the touchline, demanding to know why he'd been told to move.

'Well, Dominic's a bit bigger than you, so I thought he had more chance of getting the ball,' she smiled.

'He's not that much taller,' Davey muttered, scowling quite fiercely as he moved away.

Jakki had failed to realize just how sensitive Davey was on the matter of his height and it soon became clear that he wasn't going to forgive her. His form declined so sharply that, in the second half, she felt she had no alternative but to substitute him. She moved Sean up front as an out-and-out attacker, pushed Josh into midfield and brought on Larry Hill as a defender. Unlike Esko, who remained on the bench, Larry didn't complain to her that he was supposed to be a striker, not a full-back. Larry was just thankful to get on to the pitch. Kieren, who was standing beside his mum when she made her changes, didn't pass any comment. He didn't think they'd work, but it was nothing to do with him. In any case, much of the time his mind was on Andi, still at home recovering from her injury.

Friday Bridge were as delighted to get a draw as the Kings were dismayed. Once again, Jakki felt slightly comforted that her team had gained a point. At some stages in the match, particularly in a bright spell late in the first half, they'd played with something of their old flair. It simply hadn't lasted and towards the end they were hanging on for dear life against a real battering from the Friday forwards.

She wished she could discuss the game and tactics and attitudes with someone, but there wasn't anyone she could ask. It was unfair to try to involve Kieren in discussions about his team-mates and, sadly, Jane Allenby again wasn't present at the match. If she'd decided to give up on the Kings altogether then Jakki could hardly telephone to ask her advice. So she must continue to go it alone as coach.

She thought things were getting better when the Kings started really well against their next opponents, the gold-shirted Skeefling Swifts. On another mild morning, and playing on a fairly slushy pitch, they were a goal up after just two minutes, Reuben shooting crisply from close range following some hard running by Sean. Within five minutes the lead should have become 2–0 when Josh had a free header from a corner. Inexplicably, he sent the ball soaring over the bar, to the obvious relief of the Swifts' coach.

The Kings continued to dominate, but couldn't convert chances into goals. Jakki tried to work out what she could do to remedy this situation but it was almost half-time before she reached a decision. So, at the interval, she took Dominic aside and suggested he wasn't contributing as much to the game as he should be.

'What d'you mean?' he asked suspiciously.

'You're staying too far back. You're playing as a striker – that's what you said you wanted. But you're not getting into the box, Dom, which is where you've been needed.'

His eyes narrowed and he flicked his mane of reddish hair, always a sign that he was in an argumentative mood. 'I'm drawing my marker out of position, aren't I? So there's a gap that Josh can cut through when he gets the ball. That's what we're planning.'

'Oh,' was all she could reply immediately. Then she pointed out: 'But Josh is a defender. He's not a striker now.'

'He's not defending all the time, is he? He's playing as a sort of sweeper. When he can get forward, he does,' Dominic stated confidently. 'That's why there's got to be an opening for him.'

Jakki really had no idea how to counter that argument and so she simply nodded and let Dominic rejoin the rest of the players. Was this a tactic that had been devised by Dominic's mum, she wondered. That was perfectly possible, because Jane had developed a reputation as a soccer strategist. Kieren had told his mum that Mrs Allenby had gained her knowledge from football books and magazines and watching the game on TV; she also had made a point of chatting to other coaches and even referees at matches when that was possible. Although she didn't really know Dominic very well, mostly because he didn't socialize as much as some of the others, she suspected that he was quite a thinker himself, so maybe he had worked out his own plan for this match.

Midway through the second half she was able to congratulate herself on getting one thing right. When Frazer's gallop along the left wing was brought to a full-stop by a sweeping tackle she had someone who could attend to any injury he might have sustained. Robert, a friend, was a local builder and he'd taken a couple of first-aid courses because, he said, medical knowledge was always useful in his trade. So Robert trotted on to the pitch with his bag of sponges and treatments and Frazer was quickly on his feet again, looking no worse for what had been a spectacular tumble.

While Frazer was being attended to she'd noticed Esko start another run along the touch-line as if warming up in case he were needed. Jakki bit her lip. Should she put him on as a substitute? He hadn't impressed her with his attitude at the last match but he'd worked hard in training. She didn't know what to make of the polite, stylish boy with the straw-coloured hair, feeling that any player would surely be glad to get into a game, whatever position he was asked to take up. That was something she could have asked Kieren about, but he claimed he didn't want to talk football with her while he was suspended. He'd be back for the next match, however.

With the ref already having looked at his watch she was sure they'd secured the points for a rare away win when, disastrously, Larry Hill pushed the ball back to his goalkeeper from just outside the box. Icy plainly hadn't expected it and was slow to move off his line to kick it downfield. The ball slowed in the mud and that was enough for a Swifts' striker to live up to their name, swooping on the ball and steering it well wide of the advancing Icy. Where he'd got the energy from at this late stage of the game Jakki simply couldn't imagine.

So, for the third match in succession, the Kings had to settle for a draw. 'Tough luck,' Robert commiserated. 'Your lads deserved better. They looked pretty good at times.' She thanked him for that but couldn't go along with it. The play had been very patchy and the Kings weren't playing even half as well as they had under Jane's leadership. They no longer *looked* like a team; they may all have been playing in the same purple-and-white strip, but they performed like a collection of individuals. What on earth could she do to weld them into an effective unit again?

During the following week she resisted the impulse to telephone Jane and ask her to help out. That simply wouldn't be fair, because there was no doubt Jane would say yes, even though she might not want to: her loyalty to the Kings would be paramount, Jakki believed. She had to solve the problems on her own, or give up the job altogether. A bonus for the home game with Bowlacre Shots was that Kieren would be resuming his role in defence and would captain the team again. She consulted Oats about that and he'd insisted that Kieren should be skipper again. 'I've not led us to victory and K has, so it's got to be him, Mrs Kelly,' he declared. 'Oh, and maybe he'll bring us a bit of luck again. Everything's been going against us recently.' Jakki appreciated the fact that he didn't add 'since you took over as coach'.

For what seemed like hours she pondered what changes, if any, to make to the line-up. With Kieren's return, Larry Hill could go back to the subs' bench and that, she believed, was a plus sign. She asked Dominic if he'd prefer to revert to his old defender's role but he replied that he wanted to stay where he was. 'I'm sure I'll get a goal for us, honestly,' he said, almost pleadingly. She nodded and had her fingers crossed. Once again she considered whether she should introduce Esko into the defence at some stage, for she sensed that if he wasn't involved soon he might well abandon the Kings and try to find another team.

She was just about to go into the dressing-room for the pre-match pep talk when she spotted Jane entering the ground and so she went to greet her. 'Really good to see you again, Jane,' she enthused. 'We've all missed you. I didn't ring because I felt it might be unfair. You might want to have a complete rest from football. Wouldn't blame you!'

'Oh no, nothing like that,' Jane assured her. 'I kept away because I thought it would be unfair on you if you had your predecessor hanging around, scrutinizing everything you do. I've missed the Kings, I can tell you, so it's great to be back. I hope we're going to have a good win today, for everyone's sake.'

They chatted a little longer about recent events until Jakki realized that if she didn't hurry she'd be too late for her final words to the team. And because she was in a rush she didn't knock before she went in. The hubbub dropped immediately the boys saw who it was and the phrases she'd rehearsed were on her lips before she realized something was wrong. She hadn't focused on anyone in particular but suddenly she noticed that two of the boys weren't wearing anything at all and one of them, Danny, had just emerged from taking a pre-match shower, a new habit of his, even though he wasn't likely to be playing in this game. For a moment she paused, uncertain what to do. Then she heard Kieren hissing his disapproval: 'Muuuuum!'

'Sorry, sorry!' she called, flustered, as she made her rapid exit. Her embarrassment, she guessed when she'd calmed down, would be no greater than that of the boys themselves. The best thing to do now, she decided, was to say nothing about it and hope the players would forgive her.

They all appeared to avoid her eye as they emerged from the dressing-room to face the Shots. All she could do was wish them luck and urge them to 'Play at your best!' It wasn't much of a rallying cry.

Bowlacre, in their shirts of red-and-blue hoops on a white background, were a neat and nippy side. Knowing very well what a poor run of form the Kings were in, they began in confident style, switching the ball about from wing to wing and keeping the Kings penned in their own half. To Jakki's dismay, Kieren made an early blunder, failing to trap the ball from a pass from Joe and then stumbling as he went in pursuit of the opponent now in possession of it. He cleverly outwitted Frazer before lifting it towards his fellow striker. Only a good leap from Harry Greenland when the attacker tried a snap header prevented Bowlacre from taking the lead. Gratefully clutching the ball, Harry took his time before kicking it far upfield.

'He's managing to send it further, now; he's really improving,' remarked Danny, who had come to stand midway between her and Jane Allenby on the touchline. In previous matches, she recalled, he had watched from behind the Kings' goal, or even from the other side of the pitch.

'Er, yes, I'm sure you're right, Danny,' she responded. Moments before he spoke she'd been wondering whether she'd made a mistake in bringing Kieren back into the team so soon after his suspension. Now her mind returned to the unfortunate situation in the dressing-room.

Then, to even their own surprise, the Kings took the lead. Dominic had won a corner on the right and Reuben, as usual, took it left-footed to swing the ball in to the goalmouth. The keeper jumped, punched the ball instead of catching it and then, landing off-balance, stumbled and fell. There was a mêlée as every-one tried to gain possession until Reuben, running in at top speed, hit the ball with power. His luck was in, for the shot evaded everyone and flashed into the far corner of the net.

The lead lasted barely a minute. Bowlacre retaliated with a penetrating break down the left flank. Once again, Kieren failed to control the ball when Frazer intercepted a cross and nodded it towards his skipper. The Shots' striker pounced, looked up, let fly and leapt in delight as the ball rocketed into the top of the net. Harry hadn't moved because there'd been no warning. Both goals seemed to have come almost out of nothing. Jakki was in turmoil; no sooner had something good happened to the Kings than everything went wrong again. Had

Kieren suddenly become a liability? If so, should she take him off?

She glanced along the touchline, wondering whether to seek Jane's advice. But she couldn't yet bring herself to do that. Life, she reflected, had been so much easier when she was in the pop-music business. All she had to do then was tell her manager what she wanted; usually, she got it. Now, she couldn't see what was wanted to improve the Kings' performance.

'Come on, boys, get it together!' she called, clapping her hands just to make a positive statement. Nowadays, no one was chorusing 'Kings rule!' The Kings were being overthrown by the opposition.

Yet they still had the energy and enterprise to take the lead again just before half-time. Once again, Reuben was both the provider and the finisher. He went off on one of his many runs, twisting sinuously past every challenge and obstacle before exchanging a delightful one-two with Sean. Then, much sooner than the goalie expected, Reuben fired in a shot that was just too hot for him to handle. It actually rebounded from the keeper's chest and Reuben, following up, had the simplest of tasks to sweep the ball into the net.

'That was wonderful, Reuben; you're playing brilliantly – well, you all are,' Jakki told her team at the interval. They all knew that wasn't true but no one said anything. Kieren wouldn't even look at her. Having said that, she could hardly make any changes unless there was an emergency.

There wasn't an emergency, merely another setback, one that was to have long-lasting consequences for the Kings. Late in the second half Joe Parbold took another knock on the head that left him looking distinctly groggy. Robert ran on to administer treatment and then reported that, although the central defender appeared to be unhurt, it might be best to substitute him before long in case he suffered delayed concussion. 'Oh, I'll give him a minute to see how he reacts,' Jakki replied.

That indecision was fatal. Bowlacre, attacking briskly down the middle, won a free kick on the edge of the box. The ball went high into the wall, Joe couldn't get his head out of the way and as he collapsed in a heap the ball looped high over everyone, including Harry, and fell into the back of the net. Rodale Goal

Kings 2, Bowlacre 2. And that was the final score.

As her players trooped dejectedly towards the dressing-room Jakki saw that Joe was again receiving some attention from Robert. Jane was there, too, plainly offering advice.

'Robert and I agree that he needs to be checked out at the hospital, make sure nothing's been damaged. I've got the car with me, so I'll take him if you like, Jakki. You'll want to go and commiserate with the team, won't you? Bad luck, really, they deserved to win today.'

'I haven't won a game yet,' Jakki murmured. 'Four draws – that's no good. We need to *win*.'

'Oh, your luck'll change; bound to,' Jane smiled. 'You've got to believe in yourself. Anyway, I'll whisk Joe off to Casualty. Must say, *his* luck doesn't alter much. It was when he played rugby that he broke his nose, poor lad. See you, Jakki.'

Jakki waited until everyone had gone before deciding what to do. Then she turned towards the car park. She simply couldn't face the idea of entering the dressing-room now. There was nothing she could say that would help anyone.

'Now listen, guys, I'll do the talking,' Kieren said firmly to his team-mates as they assembled outside Dominic's house. 'I'm the captain and it'll be my mum we're discussing. But if anybody else has got something really *important* to say, then say it. I mean, we've got to convince her we all think the same way. That we *need* her to save us. Dom, what about you? If she agrees, then you'll be back in the same position I've been in. How d'you feel, mate?'

Dominic shrugged. 'I can live with it, I suppose. But she won't want me up front any more, I'll tell you that. You'll be back as main striker, Davey, that's for sure.'

'Good,' Davey responded, eyes gleaming. He didn't have to add anything because they all knew how desperate he was to start scoring goals again for the Kings. If they had to take a secret vote on who they all regarded as their most ambitious team-mate, Davey would win by a distance.

They were about to move up the path when Frazer said quietly: 'Just something we've got to think about, K. We've all got to be kind to your mum. She did her best for us, she wanted us to win all the time. Things just haven't worked out, that's all. She's been kind to us, so we've got to be decent to her.'

'That's how I feel, too,' murmured Reuben. One or two nodded in agreement but no one else spoke. Most of them were just wishing that this extraordinary meeting with Jane Allenby could be over and done with as soon as possible.

Kieren, however, felt he must re-emphasize one thing before they went in. 'We *are* going to be kind to my mum. That's definite. We'll be doing her a big favour. You know what I told you she said to me and my dad only last night. She said she feels "a wreck because of all the nervous tension I'm feeling". Afterwards dad told me any other coach or manager would have said "pressure", because that's what it is. So after this she won't have that any more. She'll be happy. She'll be my normal mum again.'

Even though Dominic was among the group and could have admitted them all to the house without the need to knock on the door, Kieren decided it was only fair to let Mrs Allenby see who was calling. Then, if she didn't want them inside, she could say so.

'Oh, how nice to see you all!' she exclaimed when she opened the door. Her astonishment was as obvious as her smile. 'Please do come in. To what do I owe this honour?'

As soon as they were all gathered in the sitting-room, perched on the edges of chairs and the arms of the sofa, Kieren made the announcement he had rehearsed several times, the announcement his team-mates who were present completely supported.

'Mrs Allenby, we all want you to take over as our coach again. We need you. We all agree about that. We –'

'But –' she was starting to say when Dominic interrupted her.

'Mum, please just listen to Kieren,' he requested. 'We've thought about everything and we're behind him. Everyone who's here, I mean.'

She nodded her understanding and Kieren resumed. 'I know how my mum feels. We've talked about it. She wants to pack in being the coach because it's not working for her. She told me and dad she thought she wanted it, but now she realizes it's not for her. She admits she doesn't know enough about football, not like you. So she'd like to resign but she doesn't know who would take over. We think if she knew you'd do it again she'd pack up immediately. So, will you? *Please*?'

For a moment or two, Jane didn't make any response at all. Dominic could tell that his mum wasn't as calm as normal, yet he had no idea what was going through her mind. He felt he should add something that would help.

'Mum, Kieren's right. You know best how to organize us and . . . and *motivate* us. I'll move back into defence and Davey can go back to leading the attack and all that, just as it used to be. We won the Championship with you in charge. We want you to be in charge again.'

'I'm touched, really touched,' Jane said, after another brief pause. 'I need to think about it. I need to think things through. Think about *everything*. I've also got to have a word with Jakki. That's very important. I accept what you've told me about your mum, Kieren, but I will have to talk to her myself. That's only fair to everybody. After that, I'll make a decision. So, boys, I'm afraid I can't give you an answer right away. But I'm very, very flattered that you've asked me.'

With that, the deputation of Kings had to be content for the present.

7 *The Will to Win*

The Goal Kings came out running. They emerged from the home changing-room with more enthusiasm and at a faster speed than they'd previously shown at any time during their so far lacklustre season. Some of their fans were so impressed they actually began to chant 'Kings rule! Kings rule!' That was a sound that hadn't been heard in Rodale Kings for a long time, hardly surprisingly, because the football club was almost at the very foot of their divisional table in the Highlea Sunday League.

Jane Allenby smiled, thinking that might be a happy omen. She'd also seen that the opposition, Kellington, were wearing their usual strip of green with green-and-white hooped socks. Green was definitely her lucky colour, so perhaps her luck was really going to be in today. It needed to be: it would be terrible to start her second spell as the Kings' coach with a home defeat. Already several supporters had come up to wish her luck and express their pleasure that she was in charge of the team again. For their sake, and that of the players themselves, she just had to succeed this time.

When Kieren won the toss and elected to play towards the favoured cricket pavilion end that, too, appeared to be a sign that all would go well for them. Danny strolled up to stand beside her on the touchline and she was pleased that he was there in what had become a familiar arrangement. To complete the picture, she felt that Jakki should have been there, too, to offer her comments and support. Understandably, however, Jakki had told her in one of several telephone conversations during the previous few days that she felt it best to miss the first half of the match but she hoped to be along later. Jane appreciated that tactful move.

Within seconds, the Kings had launched an all-out attack on the Kellington goal. Sean tigerishly fought for and secured possession in midfield and then released the ball with perfect timing for Reuben to set off on one of his mazy runs that took him practically into the penalty area. A crude tackle brought the Kings a free kick which Reuben himself took, flighting the ball cleverly across the box for Josh to climb high and head for goal. The keeper, however, was well placed to catch the ball at the top of his jump and then boot his clearance to the half-way line. Josh grimaced. He felt he should have done better. A goal then would have been the perfect way to signal his return to the team's strike force. Still, it had drawn some cheers from Kings' fans and he saw that Jane, too, was applauding. He thought it might be for him.

Although that wasn't an isolated attack by the home side it was soon Kellington who were dominating the exchanges. Their brightest talent was a strongly built, dark-haired striker called Marc Ellander, who quickly seemed to be involved in every move his team made or attempted. His strength enabled him to hold off opponents determined to take the ball off him and before long his purposeful runs through the middle began to unsettle the Rodale defence. Clearly, he was capable of causing havoc and Jane wondered whether to change her system and put a permanent marker on him. Joe Parbold would have been the ideal candidate but unfortunately The Rock was still recovering from concussion and she doubted that his replacement, Gareth Kingstree, would do such a good job on Kellington's star player.

While she was still considering this, Kellington scored. Or, to be strictly accurate, the Kings conceded an own goal. Another bustling Ellander charge into the box was almost halted when Kieren and Oats together went to dispossess him. Clearly, Marc thought he could still get past them until Kieren's foot caught his ankle. Frazer, seeing the ball run free and Icy still crouched on his line, flung himself forward to steer the ball away from danger. But all he succeeded in doing was hooking it past his goalkeeper and into the net by the far post.

Frazer rolled to his feet, horror on his face. As the jubilant Kellington forwards wheeled away in triumph Kieren went across to console his team-mate. 'Could have happened to any one of us. Forget it, Oats, just forget it.' Of course, that was impossible. Still, Jane, who'd heard his words, signalled her support.

That setback was bad enough. Worse was to follow within sixty seconds. Wasim was one of Kellington's wingers and his electric pace hadn't been revealed before Marc sent him on his way with a gem of a long pass. The Kings, inevitably after just giving away a goal, were attacking in force and so the defence was non-existent. Wasim really had no one to beat as he sped on and the referee was ignoring all appeals for offside. Icy barely hesitated before advancing, but Wasim was cool enough to slow fractionally and then slide the ball wide of him from the edge of the box into the yawning net. Goal Kings 0, Kellington 2.

Jane closed her eyes at the awfulness of it all. Had she made the worst mistake of her life in agreeing to return as coach? Were the Kings beyond her kind of help, or even any kind of help? She couldn't believe that. She opened her eyes.

By half-time, Kellington hadn't added to their lead, but neither had the Kings reduced the deficit. Thankfully, they hadn't shown signs of panic or despair. They'd continued to play well and intelligently without finding a way of breaking down Kellington's well-organized defence. It was obvious now that the visitors were content to sit on their lead and go home with the points.

'It's not all over, that's the important thing,' Jane told her boys. 'I'm not making any changes yet because you're all playing pretty well. Just remember what I told you at the start of the season: 2–0 is always a dangerous score. If you can nick one goal back you're always in with a chance; score two and they're rocking, they're desperate to hold on. Then they're vulnerable. Go back out there, Kings, and prove you can do it!'

Reuben, she believed, might have the key to unlock Fortress Kellington and indeed it was he, combining smartly with Sean, who created the first attack of the second half. A through ball from him sent Davey on his way through the middle until sheer numbers halted his progress. For once, Davey hadn't sensed when he needed to pass and so Josh was the one who felt most frustrated after yelling for the ball. Reuben, however, was the one to suffer most.

By now, Kellington had seen how effective the blond-haired playmaker was at setting up chances. So, the next time he had the ball was the last: Marc charged in recklessly and received a yellow card. Reuben's right knee took the brunt of the challenge and the pain was dreadful.

The ref himself helped the injured boy to the touchline, where Jane's exploring fingers discovered no obvious damage in the knee. All the same, he couldn't be allowed to continue, even after a pain-killing spray had been applied. Jane looked round to make a substitution and saw Jakki Kelly approaching with Andrea McKinnon. They'd arrived at the ground in time to see the incident and wanted to help.

'We'll take him to the dressing-room if you like, Jane,' Jakki offered, 'and look after him. Get him to lie down.'

'I know a bit about knee injuries after what happened to me,' Andi added. 'I'll help if you like.'

'I'm grateful,' Jane said, and meant it. 'Means I can concentrate on the match. Reuben, don't worry. I'm sure there's no serious damage.'

Tears were in his eyes but he managed to keep them at bay as he nodded at her. 'Hope we hit back at them.' With his arms round their shoulders, and limping heavily, he was half-carried to the comfort of the dressing-room.

'Esko, I want you to take Reuben's place,' Jane instructed the eager substitute. 'Just play as he does. I know you can. I've seen what you can do in training. Just link up with Sean and target Davey and Josh. Give Davey the ball in space and he'll do the rest.'

Marc Ellander, with one caution to his name already, was almost half-hearted in his tackle when he challenged Esko the first time the Finnish boy received the ball. That was a mistake he wouldn't forget. For Esko neatly hurdled the outstretched leg, regained posession and started to accelerate. That encounter was just inside the Kellington half and it was still a long way to goal. Nobody in the visiting team suspected that the straw-haired, long-limbed attacker wouldn't part with the ball in the next few seconds. That was another mistake that wouldn't be forgotten. Esko's change of pace defeated two opponents, his sharp swerves, first this way, then that, outwitted two more. Davey was sprinting to take a parallel course, expecting any moment to get the pass he craved. Esko ignored him, slowed up, darted forward again and now was on the eighteen-yard line itself. Kellington's keeper had been casually patrolling his area while watching proceedings without any sense of anxiety. Suddenly, he realized he ought to retreat as his co-defenders failed to stem the attack. But he was too late.

Esko paused again, his back-lift was minimal and his accuracy was perfection. His right foot went under the ball and lifted it high over the keeper's head to send it in a lazy kind of loop into the back of the net. It was a goal of such stupefying skill that for some moments hardly anyone reacted. Then, as the cheers rang out from all the Kings' supporters, even Kellington fans felt they had to applaud such brilliance from a player who hadn't even been on the pitch five minutes earlier.

'WOW! What a fantastic goal!' Jane exulted.

'Fantastic!' echoed Danny, himself well remembered as the scorer of a spectacular goal for the Kings when playing out of goal. Jane wasn't going to say so, but she regarded Esko's as in a different class altogether.

As soon as he'd been released from his team-mates' ecstatic embraces Esko set about proving that nothing he'd performed so far was a fluke. His advantage over Reuben was that he used both feet equally well, so he was as happy on the right flank as the left. Instinctively, Sean and the defence fired passes at him whenever opportunities arose, and when the ball wasn't actually coming towards him Esko raced in search of it. Soon, Jakki returned to stand on the touchline and watched in awe as the substitute took control from everyone else.

'He's an absolute revelation,' she murmured to Jane. 'I see now where I went wrong. I never gave him his chance. Didn't have any idea he was this good.'

'Don't worry, nobody else did, either,' Jane smiled. 'Though Dominic kept telling me Esko could do wonderful things in training. He hasn't pushed himself forward, either. Been very patient. Oh, how's Reuben?'

'Seems happy enough. The pain's more or less gone and he's swapping stories of injured knees with Andrea. So I left them to it.'

Inevitably, Kellington were falling back all the time, worried that they were going to surrender their lead. Two of their players were attempting to mark Esko out of the game. Just as inevitably, that was providing increased chances for the rest of the Kings' strike force. Even so, it was Esko, before he was sent tumbling by sheer weight of numbers, who supplied the ideal through pass for Davey. With Kellington's defence in disarray, Davey sprinted towards the box, exchanged a brisk one-two with Josh and then hit the ball with all his power before the goalkeeper expected a shot of any kind. The ball whistled into the net well wide of his inert arm.

'Oh, yes, Davey, well done!' Jane applauded. 'That's just so typical of him, isn't it, that kind of goal?'

'Absolutely,' agreed Jakki, wishing he'd scored one like that during her reign as coach. Still, all that mattered was success for the Kings. Now, with full-time not far away, they were on level terms with the opposition. Well, she supposed, five draws in a row was definitely success of some sort.

By now, Kellington were fearing the worst and some of their challenges and tackling were attracting stern warnings from the referee. Marc Ellander was told in ringing tones that if he offended once more for any reason he'd be redcarded. Josh, who'd been his victim, was hobbling painfully. Jane managed to catch his attention and asked if he wanted to come off.

'No, no, we've got to win this one, Coach,' he insisted.

Jane, swapping smiles with Jakki, remarked: 'Nothing wrong with this team's spirit, is there?'

'Nothing at all,' Jakki agreed. 'You've got them playing in great form.'

Already watches were being studied and the away supporters were calling for the ref to blow the final whistle. Time had to be added on, though, for the delays caused by the injuries to Reuben and a Kellington midfielder and a knock Kieren suffered. 'Come on, Kings, one last effort,' Jane was pleading silently. If they could win after being 2–0 down then all her faith in them would be justified. Her return as coach would not be in vain.

Undeterred by opponents around him, Esko

charged forward again, scattering one or two, outwitting the others. He must have given everyone the impression that he was intent on grabbing another solo goal. But then, barely a metre from the Kellington box, he flicked the ball almost nonchalantly sideways to Sean. Not really expecting a pass, Sean for once failed to control the ball instantaneously and when it ran away from him he had to stretch for it; and that caused him and an over-eager defender to fall in a tangle.

The claims for a penalty were vociferous, especially from the players, but the ref didn't respond immediately; instead, he just stalked round the spot on the edge of the box where the incident took place, waving away players from both sides while he made his mind up. Jane had her fingers crossed for the perfect end to the match she saw as a new beginning.

The decision suited no one: it was a free kick, not a penalty. 'Hard luck,' said Jakki to no one in particular as Sean waved his team-mates into the goalmouth as he lined up his kick. Josh, tallest of the Kings, was jostling with a pair of defenders practically on the goal-line, but he wasn't Sean's target. To the dismay of many supporters he seemed to be taking his time and so there were frantic calls for him to hurry up. At least one spectator was pointing out that the ref was already raising his whistle towards his lips.

Sean could be a perfectionist and this time his kick went precisely where he intended it. Esko rose with unmatched timing and headed the ball down to where Davey was loitering. In spite of desperate tugging and shirt-pulling that was going on all around him, Davey took off, hooked his right foot round the ball and blasted it towards the goal. A Kellington shoulder got in the way but that merely diverted the ball higher and into the roof of the net.

'YES!' the Kings screamed with delight as they grabbed Davey for the celebrations. Kellington protested heatedly but the ref wouldn't hear a word against the scoring of the goal. Instead, with a shrill blast, he signalled the end of the match without the need to kick off again.

Jakki had flung her arms round Jane for a celebratory hug and kept telling her: 'Well done, well done. We've won again at last. Thanks to you.'

'Thanks to the *players*,' Jane insisted. 'What a finish! It may have looked like an own goal, but Davey will be sure to claim it!'

Kieren was busy congratulating every member of his team and punching the air with joy before waving to the Kings fans. Then, after taking a quick look round to try and spot Andrea, he darted across for a word with Jakki, who was standing alone.

'What a game, what a finish,' he gasped, unconsciously echoing the coach. 'Mum, that really was a great idea of yours to send us round to see Jane to persuade her to take over again. It's worked. Fantastic! Thanks again, Mum.'

'Good,' was all Jakki said as she smiled to see how happy he was.

The players all crowded round Jane to share their delight with her and she got a hug from every one of them, rather to the surprise of some of the spectators. She hadn't planned to say anything important to them at this moment, but suddenly that seemed like a good idea.

'Well, you did it, you proved that you could turn the most dangerous score into a victory, so well done, every one of you,' she told them. 'We had a bit of luck today, especially at the end. For the rest of this season we've got to keep that luck – and our skills – and our team spirit. That way, we'll keep winning. We won't keep our League title this time round. But *next* season – that'll be a different story, won't it, Kings?'